Paths to Attainment

John McGovan Holmes

Published by New Generation Publishing in 2013

Copyright © John McGovan Holmes 2013

First Edition

www.newgeneration-publishing.com

 New Generation Publishing

The race chapter 1

I inserted my iron bars through the holes in my tyre, stepped inside and sat down.

"Ready steady go"! Cried the starter, my assistants gave me a gentle push over the brow of the hill, I started to roll head over heals faster and faster down the slope, as I rolled some of the competitors began to lose control of their tyres and crash into each other as they careered down the hill, some hit large boulders bounced up into the air and landed on top of others, I hit an outcrop at speed, shot skyward and outward into the air still spinning round and round, I was shouting at the top of my voice faster! faster ! As loud as I could to release the tension, I had no time to see how the others were performing, I hit the ground with a loud thud, bounced a couple of times more before rolling over again and again; suddenly someone came in front of me I thought we were going to collide we touched briefly and he fell on his side, I only had a passing glimpse of him before I rolled over him. I rolled on for a few more meters before I hit the water with a loud splash, I spread my legs to act as a break as my tyre came to an abrupt halt, fell sideways and started to drift down the river, I surfaced still reeling from my journey down the slope I had virtually no control of my faculties, somehow I managed to reach the near bank, picked up my inflated tyre inner and single oar which I would use to help me paddle across the river, all the time the spectators chanting their respective candidates names over and over again

Still reeling from my down hill excursion, I sat on my tyre and started to paddle, I paddled around in circles getting even more confused I stopped for a moment to regain my composure and bumped into one of the other competitors, we were laughing all the time but serious about our goal, I shouted out aloud Rupp! Concentrate, get to grips with yourself, I regained a modicum of control over my senses, and as the haze cleared and sensibility returned I could clearly see the opposite bank and made a consertive effort to paddle in a straight line to the other side as best I could, my figure of eight style of paddling was purely mechanical as I had done this many times before, I made heavy work of it but managed to reach the other side .I berthed my inner tube, ran up the beach over the road and into the main arena to the yells of the spectators. My next task to catch one of the wild mountain goats, blindfold it, secure it by the legs and drag it across the finish line, I was still staggering and falling down getting up I bumping into one of my friends who was attempting to achieve the same result as me, I saw my quarry, he had the longest pair of horns I had ever seen and a long white beard to match, he's, for me I shouted as I grabbed hold of him by the horns he kicked out with his hind legs, and kicked one of the other entrants in the rear ,he went sprawling on his face ,I laughed so hard the tears came down my face but I held on to him for dear life ,we then proceeded to run around the arena for a what seemed like an eternity kicking and butting the air ,it was only by sheer determination that I managed to cling on even as others were ramming into me from all sides and all shouting at the top of their voices ,I dropped to my knees still managing to hang on I had a firm grip on his horns ,but he dragged me for about another ten meters ,till eventually we came to a halt as he tired ,I managed to blindfold him with my cloth, he started kicking out again ,all I could do was to hang on and hope he either tired or gave up ,"he was one mean old boy," but eventually he stopped and I managed to rope his front legs ,he dropped to his knees

4

but he was still kicking out with the back ones, I leaned heavily on his body and he fell sideways to the ground still full of life bucking as best he could even though he was well restricted ,"eventually he gave in", I secured the back legs with much effort and then tied both sets of legs together, stood up dusted myself down wiped the dust from my face ,proceeded to ascertain the situation with the other competitors who were still wrestling with their respective chosen animals ,I then proceeded to drag my prize over the finish line to a rapturous applause from the crowd ,I acknowledged their appreciation with a wave of my hand ,then dropped to my knees in complete exhaustion, as I did ,I looked up and saw my sister Meena jumping up and down shouting," that's my brother, that's my brother"!

After I had recovered my strength, I made my way to the small stage to be proclaimed the winner of the Thimi annual race which was the main attraction of the festival, I had been training hard, not for the race, but for another event that I was looking forward to participating in, I think all my hard work had given me the edge over the other competitors. That night, "I slept like a baby."

Introduction chapter 2

the Dholo race

My name is Rupp Chandra, I live in the Kathmandu valley in a small village called Thimi, because we are a rural community sometimes work is few and far between and we have to make do as best we can, we are, as children encouraged to look for work outside our own community, I am 21 years of age, 5ft 9 inches tall somewhat taller than my other relatives and the tallest of all my friends, I love kick boxing but unlike Thailand there is little or no opportunity to earn money in Nepal from such contact sports, we Nepalese are not normally renowned for our height in comparison to our European counterparts.

I live with my mother, father and younger sister Meena, a 19 year old 5ft 6 inch dark brown eyed black raven haired beauty with a face like a Bollywood film star, and as gentle as a new born lamb although at times she can be as stubborn as a mule,

My father an ex- British Ghurkha soldier, now retired ,my father has encouraged me to join the army as soon as I am old enough and this year I am old enough, we are a poor family and need to go outside our own country to maintain a reasonable life style. And the best way is to join one of the foreign armies as a recruit.

"The British are coming," "The British are coming", was music to my ears as it heralded the arrival of the recruiting staff of the Ghurkha regiments, these were the officials that would select the new intake, I have been training for months to ensure that I was fit and strong to meet the physical requirements of the tests, my father had given me advice on how to pass the physical, as the same standards for Nepalese, was required of the British themselves. Even though we are shorter in stature!

Daily for months I would run approximately 10 kilometers around the mountain tracks near to my home carrying varying loads in an old rucksack my father had given to me in order to accustomise my self to the weight required in order to carry out the arduous task, that was the main physical requirement to gain entry into the ranks of the British forces, and "now that day had come", and at last, I could try out for my dream of joining the British army, my father said; If I fail there was always next year and of course the Indian army also recruited Nepalese into their ranks. But my heart was set on the British.

My father told me that in the old days the British were not actually allowed into Nepal, and that they would wait for the new recruits in the capital Kathmandu. Their representatives would do all the necessary trials and bring the successful candidates to Pokhara; near Kathmandu for onward shipping to the U.K. Those days are gone now! and a special team from the UK comes with a mixture of British and Nepalese officers

I arrived at the football field where the British army's representatives had set up their camp, it was a good day, and although the sun was high in the sky it was warm, but bearable, I felt that if I concentrate and keep my head up I would do well.

After our details were taken we were given a paper with questions on it and told to answer as many as possible, after which they painted numbers on our chest which differentiated us from each other, as the

Europeans say" we all look alike", we were then given a back pack with weights inside surprisingly much lighter than my father had advised, they instructed us that a trail had been marked around the mountains and that we were given a time to do the course, if we completed the course within the time frame we would move on to the other tests if we completed the course outside the time then their was always next year: We did not have watches to judge our times, so it was a matter of attaining a steady pace in order not to over exert ourselves, and to complete the race in a respectable time ,so the order of the day according to my father was "steady and consistent

Introduction

We just had to run the trail and hope that we completed the course within the time limit, set by the selection committee

The road test is called the Dholo race and is run in the Kali Khola valley, the run was over familiar terrain and a route that I was familiar with I was very pleased with the lighter load, which gave me added confidence, I just concentrated on the job at hand, my concentration was absolute, and as such the passage of time flew past in the blink of an eye and before long I was back at the football field sweating hard and hoping that I was within the time frame, Chandra, "You did well "said the sergeant in charge, you can go home, but be back here at 0700 to-morrow morning to further your progress.

That night I could not sleep I tossed and turned all night checking the time afraid that I might over sleep, 7 o'clock would not come fast enough, I was up and out of the house at first light and ran all the way to the football field where I would discover if I had been successful.

We lined up, tallest to the right shortest to the left, our names were called out one after the other --- Deepak, failed Paudel failed, Magarabedi passed, Chandra passed. I felt a sudden rush of emotion happy that I had passed and would continue with my desire to succeed, but sadness for the ones that failed, but I had passed, and on my way to being a recruit in the Ghurkha company that would form part of the British army, and help my family, that was my goal and "I had succeed."! There were further tests but I felt confident that from now on it would be much easier going.

After a further six weeks of training we were bonding into a unit of soldiers the emphasis on fitness and coordination, enabling us to function and think as a single unit, aware of what the others were doing and thinking at all times and our own capabilities at the same time. New orders of the day informed us that we would be travelling to England for further more intensive training in three days time, enough time to say our farewells to our families. My father was proud my mother was sad and cried my sister Meena said she would miss me.

The flight to the United Kingdom on Qatar Airways was uneventful, most of the time I either slept or was lost in my thoughts about my family—how would they cope! How would my sister fare, without me around to protect her from the unscrupulous people that preyed on the Nepalese youngsters, but I would be earning real money,to help my family, and that was my first concern?

I reflected on the weeks of selection processes and the initial recruit training that we had experienced and that those of us that had been chosen," how lucky and proud we felt", Some of my comrades joined the Ghurkha

Contingent Singapore Police Force (GASPS) the rest of us going on for further training in England, as the new induction recruits that would make up the cadre of the newly formed Ghurkha rifles Company.

Arriving at Manchester airport we were quickly disembarked checked through

Immigration, loaded into buses and driven off to ITC (Infantry Training Coy) Catterick, to continue our training.

At ITC Catterick, we would be instructed in: learning to speak and understand the

English language and at the same time we would be instructed in the rudiments of

Soldiering, unarmed combat, light machine drills and urban warfare, all of us recruits looked forward to the training with anticipation and vigor, every one of us determined to make our families proud and to be good soldiers in the queen's army." a great honor"!

Captain Richard Keith, a tall 30 year, 6ft 2inches tall in stature, sandy blonde hair, blue eyes, had previously served two tours of duty in Iraq with the Argyle and Sutherland Highlanders where he distinguished himself during an attack by insurgent at the newly formed base in Basra for which be received the George medal and" Mentioned in dispatches".

He loved running and when the opportunity presented itself he would run with the local" Hash House Harriers," no matter where in the world he was operating in even in Iraq,in the green zone.

.Captain keith,was newly seconded to the battalion of Ghurka rifles after a year of intensive language training at ITC Catterick;was as his father before him looking forward to his new role in the battalion.His father had told him at great lengths of the bravery ,dedication and loyalty of these men from Nepal,and that" he should be proud to lead such soldiers in battle,"his arrival back at Catterick co-incided with the latest batch of recruits, ready for everything that the army could teach them,they looked as if they had just arrived from some jungle deployment with their familier bush style hats and kit bags and familiar kukri knives.

Although they spoke to each other in their local Nepali language,most understood English,as like their fathers and grandfathers before them, were serving soldiers in the British army,However, their English would be improved upon over the following 33 weeks,as would their skills as soldiers "dedicated and consienctious",and ready to form the next cadre of the Gurkha troops to be inducted into the regular British army.

Captain Richard Keith chapter 3

The product of a military family dating back to the first recorded Keith.

Robert Keith came to notoriety when he killed Cammus, a Danish invader in single combat at the Battle of Barras in Angus (Scotland) 1O1O the deed was handsomely rewarded by the King, Malcolm the second. Richard Keith had been brought up on the exploits of his famous ancestor's names such Sir Robert de Keith, who led the Scots cavalry at the battle of Bannockburn 1314, James Francis Edward Keith (1696-1755) a Field Marshal in the Prussian army, and many more famous ancestors

Capt Keith, a graduated from Sandhurst had immediately joined the Argyle and Sutherland Highlanders, after graduation where he rose to the rank of captain, he had gained recognition in Basra during an attack by insurgents where he showed a tremendously cool head under fire when confronted by a number of attackers wielding Kalashnikov AK47s (Russian assault rifles), eliminating three and taking a fourth as prisoner, the later giving vital information to the interrogation team .For his action and quick thinking he was awarded the George medal and mentioned in dispatches a recommendation which would prove an asset when applying for a commission in the regiment of Gurkha's

Capt. Keith, had just returned from Malaysia where he attend the International Hash House Harrier gathering in Kuala Lumpur, running was a passion of Capt. Keith's and he loved to run with any of the hash groups no matter where he was stationed as the Hash was an international phenomenon, which was started in 1938 in Kuala Lumpur, by the British military at the Royal Selangor Club, where the bored soldiers would run around the Padang (grassy area) and through the near by rubber plantations, the trail was marked with flour or paper depending what they had a surplus of at the time hence Capt Keith's visit. He wanted to experience the true nature of hashing in the land of its birth and experience running through the jungles and plantations of the once British colony, it would be a real contrast to pounding the pavements around Catterick, which he had been doing for the last twelve months

"The home coming"! Was the theme of the four yearly event, He felt that he deserved his holiday after a long year of studying Gurkhali at Catterick prior to taking up his new commission in the newly forming "1st Battalion of Ghurkha rifles. "He felt fresh and ready to start his new challenge, with the regiment that his father had commanded before him and whom he had nothing but the highest regards, for their bravery, loyalty and unswerving commitment to duty that was the ilk of these mercenary soldiers from Nepal A loyalty that was surpassed only by the highlanders who fought against, and with the English armies in the past." soldiers to be proud of, and proud to lead." He noted the arrival of a new intake of recruits arriving from Nepal as he strode across the parade ground to report back from his Asian, trip. and to determine his new orders.

Catterick chapter 4

Catterick would be our new home for the foreseeable future,for more basic training and english language studies.

We would be visiting the camps at Brecon beacons for cross country, survival and endurance courses,and speciality training at Romney marshes.

After we had alighted from the buses there was a bark of orders... fall in...? attention! At ease.

Major G. Brigstok, Garrison Commanding officer, will now give us a short speech on what was expected of us as British soldiers, to our surprise he spoke in Gurkhali, he said: The British Army was a truly professional army valued by the nation in which we serve, robust and useable and ready to undertake at short notice any tasks that is required of it, be it civil aid or war.

An army characterised by an ethos whose core values are: selfless commitment, physical and moral courage, self discipline and respect for others; an army which recognises the need to develop and educate its people to the highest standards that are available, as soldiers you must set a high standard, it is a matter of not what I tell you to do, but a case of leadership by example

Advancement is on an equal opportunity and individual merit and bearing this in mind the army offers a truly rewarding career to those of you who have the drive and determination to succeed in the modern army," men! With that I welcome you to your new home, for the next 24 weeks which will be the Bhandbhagta Gurung VC block here at ITC Catterick"! And that before long we will see you trained and equipped as combat infantrymen, ready for deployment to any theatre of war that requires your skills," good luck to you all,"! We all saluted and ordered to about turn and marched off to our new home for the foreseeable future.

Our accommodation block was spacious and well laid out, the beds were all in line with about 1 meter between beds, a storage locker at the side a footlocker at the bottom of the bunk very clean and Spartan, but it was home.

The first week was up at 0400 wash, breakfast, and 2 hours marching followed by rifle drill lunch and two hours on the firing ranges as the weeks passed we were becoming a cohesive force like a well oiled machine our English improving by the day all in all we were working towards well coordinated fighting machine

My first encounter with Captain Keith, was during our first night maneuvers on the ranges at Catterick, the Gurkha forces, acting as the enemy, our orders to attack a British column when they would least expect us, Captain Keith was our company CO and under his command we were to reek as much havoc as possible on a mobile battle group, thus simulating an attack by insurgents on the convoy. We were given the route the convoy would take, the convoy were expecting the attack but where and when was up to the attacking force to decide. Captain Keith, briefed us to set up an ambush situation at a corner on the route where there was an overhang where we could pick of the armoured division personnel who hopefully would rush to the aid of the first track vehicle occupants which would burst into flames when we detonated the mines that would explode and stop the lead vehicles in there tracks, causing simulated casualties following troops would rush to help, allowing us the attacking force to shoot and kill as many as possible and then spirit away in the dark with the minimum or no casualties that was the plan simple in its concept, leaving the convoy in total disarray, the scene was set, the convoy approached ,we were in position when a stray cow suddenly wandered into the road just about 50 meters from our explosive devices out of sight of the oncoming convoy, in a real situation the cow would have been an ideal distraction but it was not real it was a mock situation, and something had to be done, and quickly, in Nepal the cow is sacred to the Hindu, and this poor animal was about to be scared out of its wits when the mock battle begins, with all the noise and commotion that was about to ensue, I signalled my intention to the CO that I would run to the cow and hopefully walk it away from the coming melee to a place of safety and join the company at the designated meeting point after the attack. He acknowledge my intentions, and off I ran, the cow had its back to me so did not see me coming, thank goodness, as she might have bolted, I started to talk softly as I approached, at the same time I patted and rubbed her back, I removed my cravat wound it around her neck still talking softly, the huge tongue came out and licked my tunic and nearly lifted me off my feet, but I gently but firmly guided the cow off the road and away from the scene, jogging slowly, away from the scene, there was no moon in the sky which was a blessing as it made it difficult for the lead warrior tank commander to see me now gently running away from the site, My first taste of battle (only simulated) but here was I guiding a dumb animal out of the area. As the distance widened 500-600 meters, I knew that there was less chance of the cow bolting

I came to a small hill I led my charge behind knowing that the hill would reduce the noise from the attack and not startle the animal, suddenly! there was the muffled thuds of incendiaries going of and the sky lit up, I wrapped my cravat around her eyes and waited, after the first explosions there was the lesser noise of rifle fire a lot of shouting, but in the distance and not enough to scare the poor animal. I waited until it all settled down, took my cravat from the cow wound it around my neck said farewell to my bovine friend and made my way in the dark to our agreed rendezvous point.

I arrived at the rendezvous point before everyone else and smelling of cow as my platoon arrived they joked about my action; remarks such as "a fine time to take up farming"! Rupp Midnight cowboy, we could smell you a mile away. When the CO arrived he beckoned me over, Chandra!" You did well tonight"! the attack was successful, and we met all our objectives. Thanks to your quick thinking the plan would have been a total failure," I know that you feel bad at missing your first encounter, but believe me there will be more. "I can assure you of that"!

The comments continued as we made our way back to our de briefing at the base.

Meena's Loneliness chapter 5

Since Rupps departure to the army, Meena found that the daily chores of feeding the chickens and watering the vegetable garden became monotonous and boring and that the house was a very lonely and quiet place without Rupp .She found herself day dreaming of the day she would be strolling down the road near to the house when a rolls Royce car conveying a Bollywood mogul who was just passing by looking for a location in the village for some scenes for his latest movie, when he would spot Meena strolling along the road, he would watch her movements for a while, and be captivated by her gracefulness and beauty, instructing his chauffeur to pull over, he would exit the vehicle and introduce himself, explain to Meena who he was, He would ask to meet her father to explain his reason for coming to Nepal ,he would also express his interest in his daughter Meena and that he had a part in his new musical in which Meena with her dark beauty would be ideally suited

Father would make an agreement with the director, and an offer for Meena would be made and accepted by her father He would allow the movie mogul to make arrangements for her to go to Mumbai for training and to star in films, She would become a mega star and her picture would be all over the news and she would be featured on the billboards advertising everything from toothpaste to underwear, she would buy her parents a new house and they would be secure for the rest of their lives, She would meet a wealthy and handsome foreigner and after a period of courtship be married and go to live in America,

Alas! it was only a dream and she would be brought to reality with a bang when her mother would call for her to go to the garden and clean out the chicken coup She wondered how her brother was and hoped that a letter from him would arrive soon telling her of all the wonderful things she wanted to know about life in England, was everybody rich did they all drive cars, their clothes the food the ate, questions, question, questions, meanwhile her life was empty.

When Rupp was around she would sing and dance all over he house happy in the thought that her brother was always there encouraging her never to give up her dream as she was a wonderful singer and a graceful dancer and that she had the talent to be "a big star" and that one day her opportunity would come, but when would that happen, soon, I hope thought Meena, but it seems unlikely.

Sennybridge chapter 6

(The Brecon Beacons)*

A few days later we were advised to prepare ourselves for a trip to Sennybridge, Wales, to the famous Brecon beacons, where the terrain was just like home but the weather much, much more unpredictable.

Captain Keith informed us that our progress was on schedule and that the next step in our training required us to learn the skills of navigation and map reading across open country.

We arrived at Sennybridgelate in the afternoon in time for evening meal, paraded to our quarters,given an hour to unpack our equipment and rest before being mustered to be informed of our training schedule the next day.

Monday map reading course followed by a 2 mile run with light pack against the clock,this would be the routine for the next couple of days.the load increasing daily as was the distance until Friday when we would run individually, with half full bergen approximately 16 kg and weapons belt 17kg, and our weapon the S80 rifle.

Rifle to be kept in hand at all times,we would be given a map grid references and told to navigate by compass until we reached reference as depicted on the on the map,where upon a new set of instructions would be given so as to procede to the next objective, the object of to test to test our stamina and newly aquired map and navigation skills.

My route chapter 7

Up at 0600 Breakfast, briefing, check equipment collect maps, compass and information and check in. I was taken to map reference 5J (SN86 1318) my starting point of the exercise, from here to navigate my way to my first point of reference information at hand I started my journey, I dropped down a boundary fence ,taking care as I crossed a couple of roads ,I followed the fence line to a point 6A (SN 864319)I left the boundary here to cross above a deep gully before joining the fence line as it changes to an internal fence the weather was cold .overcast but no rain~.After a fairly flat initial 2 km stretch, the ground descended down to a bridlegate, which gave access to the bridal way network

From here I wound my way down to the Nant Gwyddering Bridge. After crossing the main river I forded a secondary stream before climbing a bank, the ground was firm so I climbed with little effort. Emerging from the river valley breathing moderately, I then found myself back at the boundary fence, which climbed up to point 6C(SN87 8322). I turned westerly beside the woods passing between two plantations to reach a further stream at (6D (878322).

From here the going got heavier as the uneven ground climbs to the corner of aplantation I noted the parachute drop zone to the west and a small lake to the east. After emerging in N Easterly direction onto firmer ground with panoramic views! Reached a high point 6E(888341) a steep down hill path to a bridge (The Nant Eithrim bridge) at Point 6F(893348.After crossing I proceeded East along a high bank to a boundary fence and then I followed it up an access road to my first staging point SN (89435 1). a quick brief of my journey a new set of directions time one hour forty five minutes. So far every thing was going well

My next phase started at7A (SN894351) I proceeded East across slightly boggy fields, across a small stream. Following the contour, passing an old derelict building and then descending to follow an old track along the side of a hill where I came to a stream, I climbed a muddy slope to reach a bridle junction Point 7A(SN 900355) breathing heavily I paused for a moment to steady my breathing.

I found the fence again and after a short distance I found a downhill track beside an old wall which I followed to a small ford, turning sharp right (SN99063 62) I followed a fence line straight downhill crossing an old wall while continuing down to reach a tract at point 7D(SN906362). Following this track for lOOm only to cross another river on a wooden sleeper bridge.

After crossing the bridge, I struck out across the open field over a small hump,

passing through a hedge, rounding above a burial mound crossing a track to reach an old stone building and ford a small stream. I turned right crossed another stream before veering left at point 7E(SN920359). Here I avoided the fence line and began to climb up to the road that cuts across the common (access) land to the South boundary point7F (SN924363) where the path skirts a plantation.

I headed north crossing a stream and then I followed an internal fence rounding a corner where the path dropped down to more fords. after crossing the fords I took a sharp turn NE which brought me to a gate in a woodland path, at the end of this path the Nant Bran Bridge is visible at point 7H(SN929372) .1 climbed up the opposite bank to a track I crossed the track through a hole in the fence and climbed steeply up.

At the top of the hedge I turned left and followed a fenced section along an old track, I continued via a bridle gate to approach the boundary fence yet again which I followed via yet another gate to reach a high point 7J(SN944376).

My route chapter 7

I almost walked into a bog to avoid it I detoured wide for about lOOm then turned back again near a very prominent tree skirting another burial mound at 7K(SN95 1 379) here I could see the firing ranges, after crossing another boggy section I started to descend cutting across corners to pass through fenced woodland emerging near a ruin. Following down to the left of a hedge towards a bridge

The next staging post came into view 7N (SN 966383). Another debriefing new instructions time on this section less than three hours. At this point I decided that a short rest and some food and water were the order of the day. I recapped on my journey so far and to determine which direction was next, one look at my instructions told me that. Westerly was the indication, I realised that I was about to go into the live firing area I hope the guns are silent to-day! Of course they would be, as to-day there would many soldiers traversing the area the same as me.

Feeling rested I set out following my new instruction, through the fence across down the grassy slope to the river, no crossing so in an effort to keep my feet dry I threw a few rocks between the larger boulders to cross without getting wet, up the bank to the other side, the going was much easier now I continued at a steady pace with very little in the way of obstacles for the next (4km) mostly moor land with shell craters dotted over the landscape, The weather started to close in, the wind was driving the rain straight at me forcing me to wipe my face constantly in a way , reminding me of home ,I passed my check points with little difficulty and started to yomp half running half bouncing ,Suddenly the silence was broken with what sounded like a voice or a red wing calling to his mate, indistinguishable at first, but becoming more and more audible, a bright orange item caught my eye my first thought was a parachute ,but as I neared 'the shape of a small human took shape, a woman! What was she doing here! as I arrived I could she was holding here ankle and moaning, what happened? What are you doing here? are you in pain?

But it was clear that she bad a badly twisted or broken ankle the result of going into a hole,or falling over, she was crying from the pain and said that she had simply gotten disorientated due to the weather and couldn't determine where she was, cold and wet I rubbed her hands gave her a gobstopper for the sugar content for energy found some sticks ,made splints with the bandages in my Bergen, and tied them around her ankle, I initially considered leaving her ,but dismissed the idea as hypothermia was setting in ,on the other hand I had been going for some time and decided that the next check point at SN (872412) was closer than the last one and if I force her to walk with my support and encouragement we could reach safety quicker. I checked my maps took a bearing and off we went, I kept asking her questions, where do you come from? what were you doing here? just simple question to keep her from going to sleep, and keeping her alert, her adrenalin had kicked in and the pain had lessoned We stumbled on talking and singing to keep her spirits up, we had gone less than 1km when we arrived at my next checking point which was beside an old military road. The steward was surprised, immediately sized up the situation and called for an air ambulance took her inside the military trailer out of the weather, and sat her down to take the weight off her leg. I explained what had happened and my decision forwarded my usual de-brief, new instructions given, I rested for five minutes before going on. Time just over two hours I was surprised I had been out for seven hours and felt reasonably fresh even after my encounter with the young lady.

The next stage of my exercise was taken up with the events of the past hours that I was crossing pleasant moor land filled with wild flowers of all description varying shades of green which had a similar feeling to home, the going was easy, I was making good time, the weather had eased the sun came out briefly and sky larks were singing at the top of their voices, I reached a heavily wooded area my next reference 4C(SN861399) I headed down a very muddy, track in a tree lined culvert, where I turned easterly down to a small ford, crossed it before turning south, here I climbed up to towards some old buildings, breathing heavily again, turning south easterly and still climbing I eventually reached a gate at 4D(862392) I continued down to a crossroad I twisted and turned for a while until I arrived at an old ruined homestead at point 4F(862383).

My route chapter 7

Heading in a Southerly direction I climbed up to the higher ground which afforded spectacular views across Carmarthenshire I continued on down the West side of a planted forest block to reach my final reference point on this phase 4G(85 8368)

Reference time one hour forty minutes the adjudicator was waiting, took my debrief, handed over my final set of instructions and informed that I had one more section to complete. 1 was tired but elated only one more trail to complete. Shucrea! Shucrea!

(Thank you) (Thank you) I said to myself god is taking care of me. I started out across open country, passing an old site of some kind I followed a track crossing a couple of streams before climbing up again to what looked like cross- country driving area The area was well rutted, the result of the 4x4 vehicles tearing up the ground, the route ahead was clear as I pushed onward at a steady pace, down a gradual incline to point 5A(895368) at the corner of a planted forestry block. I proceeded north easterly to a point 5B(860369 Following an old sheep track down to a gap in a fence at a corner dropping down to cross an old road cross a bridge near to the old fort of Clawdd Brythonig, following an old lane up to turn East through a bridle gate then along a hard track for 2 km of easy walking.

I left the track at point SD (SN 857352), proceeded along a grassy lane, and crossed a stream to reach a gate. This was an ancient bridle path a sign saying (Site of Special Scientific Interest) keeping close to the fence line for about lOOm continuing along the track to pass through a gateway at a point 5E(SN85 6345) I left the track here to climb up to the corner of the field and made a "u" turn onto a grassy track leading East up to a crossing at point 5G(SN856345) I followed the route for South Westerly for 5OOm into a forest, I continued up the forest track to reach a high point .It was a long haul and my load made me breath very heavily I was beginning to feel the strain of the days outing, I slowed for a while took some water and walked for a spell I had crossed to the other side of the cross-country driving area the way ahead was open moorland which passed between two forestry blocks at the end of which joined the military road which was where I started my day I was thank full to see the army trailer and standing there was Capt. Keith. I Took a final reading 5J (SN861 318) Saluted, was quickly debriefed. Removed my equipment and relaxed. Chandra," Its soldiers like you, who give the army credibility "said Capt Keith, the young woman is suffering from a badly dislocated ankle, minor frostbite brought on by exposure, however she will recover with no lasting I'll effect. She sends her grateful thanks to you! . again well done!

I was instructed to deposit my equipment in the rear of the army pajero (jeep) and sit in the back; I was then driven back to Sennybridge for a hot meal and a well-earned rest. "What a day"!

We spent a few more days at Sennybridge doing advancing, and covering techniques using the warrior and scimitar fighting vehicles as shields, representing close combat methods within enclosed and restricted areas

Our interaction with each other had reached a point where re- actions required of us in unexpected situations were instantaneous and without thought or

28

hesitation, a sure sign of battle group unity and military cohesion.

We returned to Catterick, satisfied with our progress and fitness and looking forward to completing our training and being absorbed into the newly formed 1st r battalion Gurkha under the command of Captain Keith. and our colour sergeant Jaya Gunung, who had been with us all the way since Kathmandu. A capable and experienced soldier of repute and admiration some one to look up to and be admired a soldier who led by example!" our guiding light."

Returning from Sunnybridge heralded the completion of our initial training and our acceptance into the 1 st. battalion Ghurkha rifles, this done captain Keith informed us that the brigade was to be posted to the Helmand province of Afghanistan at therequest of their newly elected head of state, Hamid Karzi as the Taliban were beingsponsored by Al Qaida to retake the country .However, first we will pay a visit to Romney Marshes for specialist training before embarkation to Afghanistan, One other notice, two promotions to lance corporal messers Chandra and Chaturbedi

Congratulations on your promotion gentlemen! collect your new stripes from the quartermasters stores.

Romney Marsh's chapter 8

The Romney marshes are situated in the South East of England in the county of Kent.

We were flown to Lydd international airport then bussed to Sir John Moore barracks, at Shornecliffe; the camp is in Folkestone close to the Hythe shooting ranges and the Romney marsh training areas.

We were scheduled for a two week training course, the onus being on search and destroy capability this being geared to urban warfare, the method of searching houses looking for hidden caches of arms that might be concealed for use by the Taliban, The Afghani refugees in England were employed by the ministry of defence to act as the local villagers in an effort to give the exercises a feel of authenticity On one such night raid we were given the coordinates to the village of Midley (TR016237)The village was so called because of its location, it was a small island village which lay in the river Rother between the larger ones of Romney and Lydd the brief was :insurgents had penetrated the village and held the local Pushtun members at gun point threatening to shoot the whole village unless they gave help to the Taliban cause. The entrance to the village was by way of a single narrow bridge approximately l8inches wide across the river the bridge was partially hidden under water at high tide, therefore the exercise was to be completed on a precisely timed schedule .the raid went of like clockwork the enemy located and routed the villagers rescued the arms haul found in a pit which was covered ,the whole operation went off without a hitch, in the darkness as we withdrew corporal Magararbedi, slipped off the narrow bridge and landed in the thick mud of the riverbed ,the weight of his equipment caused the mud to suck him down, we laughed at first! but the gravity of his situation became clear as the water started to trickle back, we tried pulling ,without success as we too! were at risk of falling into the black abyss, I recalled that the arms cache was hidden in a hole in the ground which was covered by scaffolding planks I explained to the captain that if we recover the boards place them on the river bed beside the corporal this would spread our weight and thus enable us to extract corp. Magararbedi from the mud ,"A good idea Chandra" !,we raced to the village, recovered the boards, returned, laid them out in the mud around him to help spread the weight then everyone pulled with all their strength, slowly but surely he emerged from the mud ,a little embarrassed at his mistake but a happy and thankful man ,as he explained that he did not like water, and was glad to be back on dry land, all of us caked in mud from head to foot as we returned to our barracks, glad that it was dark as our comrades would have shrieked with laughter at our state .Magararbedi, thanked us yet again, and promised that the next bhat curry was on him.

We trained over and over the same scenario's until we operated as one cohesive unit understanding what the other was thinking and acting on logic rather than impulse ,Colour .Sargent Gunung advised us that we were to return to Catterick as our specialist training was now complete

At Catterick we would be equipped for our tour of duty in Afghanistan with all the latest equipment! He also informed us that after the tour he would be selecting a team to aid him in the selection process for the new recruit intake back home in Kathmandu under the leadership of Captain Keith, A real honour for those who were chosen, an honour indeed. By now we were gaining in confidence virtually on a daily basis as our range of military skills grew and our English speaking skills also reaching a crescendo. We were excited at the prospect of real action in Afghanistan and the thought at possibly being chosen to accompany the sergeant on his return to Kathmandu for the selection of a new intake of recruits

Afghanistan deployment chapter 9

Our training in Wales coupled with our specialist exercises in the Marshes was a precursor to our groups main task of routing out terrorists in search and destroy operation against illegal poppy growing and manufacturing plants which were scattered all over the province, in Helmand, between operations we were designated the task of training the newly formed Afghani army, a task we did not look forward to as we did not speak or understand their language

The government supplied us with interpreters, who spoke a little English to help with giving instruction to their own soldiers ,it was like the blind leading the blind, after a lot of failures Capt. Keith advise us to work on a one to one basis the interpreters told to tell their soldiers just copy what, their opposite Nepalese number did at first it was just a comedy but as the days passed and weeks passed they started to get the idea ,they were soon marching together and in step ,we were winning, we started target practice the Afghanis just pointed at the targets and pressed the trigger until they emptied the magazine ,they were totally surprised when the targets that they were shooting at were recovered and shown to them they had completely missed, not one bullet had hit the target, patience was what was needed, and again we had to demonstrate over and over again until they realised that a rifle had to be held tightly close to the shoulder and the trigger squeezed slowly while aiming at the target with the use of the sights, but it did happen , even after many trials and failures .Nepalese people by up bringing are patient but the carrying on of these rural farmers sons who had never been subjected to uniformity found great difficulty in drills and the proper use of weapons tried our patience to the very limit, but our patience and endurance won, albeit slowly at first but more and more as they matured and developed their military skills, they developed into a force all be it a secondary force compared to their instructors they were a force to be reckoned with, they had the bravery of mountain lions fearless and aggressive they were also skilled in tracking in the wilderness, a worth while skill, one which would be invaluable on search and destroy missions.

Sergeant Gunung, advised us that reports were coming in of a hidden poppy field and

processing factory which had been spotted from the air, it was our job to investigate, and destroy if need be, the moral of the unit hit an all time high, action at last its what we were here for and what we were trained for, we were all excited.

The following morning after stand too, we were supplied with the new light body armour which was stored in the metal containers, staggered around our compound, told to checked our personal equipment, collect our ammunition, sort and check out our kit and be prepared for a walk in the clouds we breakfasted on the usual rice, scrambled eggs and local bread, we ate quickly, as we were anxious to get started. We started out at 0800 formed a straight line and began our march the captain and sergeant up front leading the line, as infantry we walk everywhere it was warm the sun was still low in the sky but we knew that it would get hotter as the day progressed but we were keen to see action that's what was uppermost in our minds ". The real thing at last."

Towards the afternoon we reached our objective, poppy fields hidden under camouflage netting so used as to fool the spotter planes that patrol the skies looking for just such a set up, the processing buildings were also hidden under the same netting, a very, very clever disguise, all in all a well hidden complex. Further scrutiny of the property revealed heavily armed personnel patrolling the area, not an easy target the captain called HQ and requested the services of Saxon armoured vehicles with flame thrower capability. He further instructed that the assets approach from the south of the co-ordinates and to make as much a commotion as they could to catch the attention of the guards, roger that sir, over and out. Captain Keith, ordered us to relax and to eat some food, we have a wait on our hands lads, we ate quietly and talked under our breath for the fear of being heard, but we were still some way off and we were in a commanding position on high ground enabling us to view the area all around our position. It seemed like an eternity before the radio broke the silence, this is iron lady one over, do you read me over the radio man acknowledge the call with the correct response and passed the receiver to the captain, this is Keith speaking, what have you got for me .We are south of your objective and would reach you in approximately fifteen minutes.

"Good iron lady,!" at exactly 1600, commence torching the poppies under the netting you will see the target ahead of you as described at this mornings briefing, that will give us time to move into position, your fires will alert the guards they will raise the alarm and run to the fires ,this will enable us to strike the target from the northern side ,the surprise should cause panic amongst the defenders, good luck iron lady over and out, We moved down from our position keeping the hills between us and our objective as we closed in on the complex sergeant Gunung paused and said ,Men this your first action, listen for my voice, your are professional soldiers and as the British say ,today you will gain your spurs,

Meena chapter 10

The offer from the carpet factory's representative for Meena was accepted N pr 20,000 $30) and fatherly approval given. Meena was given the address in Joparti, and instructions on how to get there ,a small amount of cash for traveling expenses,enough time to write a letter to her brother in England for her mother to post before wrapping all her worldly possessions in a sari,

It had been almost a year since her brother Rupp, had tested and been excepted for the British forces recruitment intake of 04 a long year, and although life went on the same she was developing into a beautiful young woman she had long jet black hair which fell all he way down to the back of her knees, eyes that reminded you of a tiger advancing towards you ready to strike, soft and inviting yet full of danger if you dropped your defense while being mesmerised with such wild beauty, and a figure that any Hollywood starlet would die for and all wrapped up in a sari, a beautiful sari.

She arrived at the carpet factory at around eight in the evening was welcomed by the manager and his wife who at first glance decided that Meena could be a lot of trouble if not watched, a wary eye had to be kept on this young beauty. The arrangements with her father and mother were again explained that she would remain at the factory in the week and allowed to go home on Saturday and Sunday, but must return for work on Monday. She would work from seven in the morning until six in the evening a break for lunch at noon a long day, but life in Nepal was hard but even harder if you were out of work as there is no social services to help to a great extent she felt fortunate. The prospect of being away from home did not bode well with Meena, but what could she do! Her father had accepted the payment and given his blessing, from now on she would be at their command for the foreseeable future

Meena was shown to a small room, the room was completely white, ceilings and walls alike clean and tidy, a single bed in the center a locker, for her clothes a small sink in the corner and chair at the foot of the bed, it was not what she expected but it was acceptable and that it was hers. She was shown to the toilet area which again was clean and tidy and well cared for, the smell of lavender emanated from the cubicles, nothing like the stories she had heard from the local people in the village of children working as slave labour and living in the poorest of conditions, not so at this factory.

The following morning she was taken to the weaving area of the factory where other woman were working knotting carpets or weaving the yarn .The manager explained to Meena that Nepalese carpets are unique from any other carpets available in the world markets in so much that they are knotted on rods as opposed to straight warps The warps and subsequent fringes, are made of heavy duty cotton. All carpets are washed by hand prior to shipping to improve the lustre of the wool, a typical (3 x 5) foot carpet has 80 knots per inch (172,800knots per carpet) requires about one month to hand knot and finish where a carpet the same size with 100 knots per inch takes a staggering (216,000 knots per carpet) takes 40 to 60 days to complete The carpets are made of 100% of New Zealand and/or Tibetan wool; the extra ordinary colours are achieved with specialised Swiss dyes.

After dying the carpets are dried on the roof of the factory but only in the spring, winter and autumn, but not in the summer as you know the summer brings the torrential rains. At this he directed Jothi Rama to instruct Meena in the techniques, of knotting, weaving and carding, procedures that the factory was famous for.

Rajan Parayan chapter 11

Rajan Parayan, was thirty six year old 5ft 4inch stockily built Nepali, from the back streets of Kathmandu, where he grew up, from as far back as be could remember he had no parents and he knew only the street life most of his young life he grew up either stealing or soft soaping some poor gullible fool out of their money, one way or another he new how to talk a good story, and extort money from an unlikely suspect. Growing up in the capital he flew close to the wind escaping from the clutches of the police on many occasions.

At the age of twenty he found employment in the carpet factories at Jorpati, the carpet centre of Nepal, he struggled for a number of years trying to make ends meet, a brief marriage to a young girl, but the pressure of trying to keep the wolf from the door, struggling to survive on poor wages forced him to quit and travel to India in search of more lucrative employment. It was during this quest in Chennai, India, that he met the famous surgeon, Dr. Amit Kumar, the Kidney specialist, who enlisted the help of Rajan to find donors who were willing to give up parts of their anatomy for a price.

Kumar promised him untold wealth if he could keep him supplied with willing paying clients as well, his duties would be to find prospective wealthy clients and suitable fresh willing donors, for which he would be well compensated. A much more rewarding occupation than that of which he had been used to at the carpet factory, at least now he had goals to strive for and money to be earned, real money, easy money, and he knew where there were plenty of opportunities.

Over a period of years be had become very

successful at his chosen profession; he had acquired more than fifty souls, most of whom he had offered vast sums of money, to part with one of their precious organs, only to cheat them at a latter date, after the deal had been completed. and they were minus a kidney. A number of the people of whom he had duped had informed the police, The police did not take likely to Rajans enterprise in selling other peoples organs as it was against the law. They eventually caught up with him and he was sentenced to a term of three years and a fine, under Sub -clause I of the Human Trafficking Control Act, anyone found trafficking in kidney trading could be sentenced up to a term of up to 10 years in jail and a fine of up to Nrp 500,000, Dr Kumar paid the fine of, Nrp 100,000, but that was all behind him and immediately after his release a telephone call to his ex employer to inform him of his release, and he was back in business

Detective Sergeant of Police (DSP) Magarabedi, had been informed of Parayans release and was advised by his superior that he should keep an eye on his where bouts and his activities for a time as he may lead them to Dr. Kumar, who was the most wanted man in Nepal and throughout the whole of India, Dr. Kumar, was always one step ahead of the police.

First contact chapter 12

At exactly 1600hrs the Saxon armoured fighting vehicles commenced burning the poppy fields with their flame throwers, the fields went up in flames with clouds of black smoke billowing skyward, the guards seeing the smoke started running and shouting at the top of their voices to-wards the burning fields in a bid to thwart the attackers

With blaring horns and Klaxon's booming out in our ears, we hit the buildings at the same time in a well coordinated attack, breaking down doors, tossing stun grenades into the buildings and moving on quickly to the next building repeating the process, as we went, when the grenades exploded they created loud noises and the maximum damage and rendering the occupants unconscious, the guards stopped in their tracks, realising too late! that the attack was coming from all directions, they turned on their heels and started towards the now burning buildings, firing their Kalashnikov rifles in a wild and uncontrolled manner, they emptied their magazines in a few seconds hitting nothing, we responded with a volley of independent fire killing four or five in the exchange and probably wounding a few others, the remaining guards realising that they were up against a superior force ran for their lives disappearing into the as yet un burning field, the Saxon fighting vehicles continued with their objective of destroying the complete crop all the time one of our apache helicopters circled above ready for action if needed

After our brief encounter with the enemy we swept the area to ensure that none of the guards were hiding with malicious intent when we least expected it,

Captain Keith, ordered us to search for under

ground tunnels in case the surface buildings were a mock operation intended to fool us into thinking that we had destroyed their factory when the real operation took place under ground, where upon they could restart their manufacturing at a latter date, after we had retreated back to our base, during our search a cache of some 200kilo,s of raw cocaine was uncovered giving us a sense of jubilation at winning the jackpot. No one was hurt during the operation ,and we celebrated with a drink of water from our canteens. A day that will live in our memories and a story to tell our children and grand children.

The radio crackled into life the operator answered,"its iron lady sir", as he handed the receiver to the captain. Iron lady, this is search one Keith, speaking we have destroyed the target, your assistance was much appreciated, you can return to base, we will sweep the area before returning to base, Keith out.

We returned to base full of our achievement and all expecting medals for our success, the next two weeks the raid dominated the conversations as more and more of the details of operation came to mind. The operation happened so fast but the details took weeks to unfold

I received a letter from my sister Meena, which surprised me. She wrote:

Dear brother,

It has been a year over since I last spoke to you, before you left to go to England to continue your military training, I hope that you are well and enjoying your new found career, father has accepted a sum of money for me, and I am to be allowed to go to Joparti to the carpet factory to learn the processes of carpet making, they have allowed me to write to you this letter before I go. I will be allowed to visit mother on weekends, but only briefly as it's a long way to and from the factory by bus. I worry that the stories that I have heard of slave labour and children working all hours and sleeping where they fall, are not true.!, since you left the house has been very quiet and 1 long to see you again brother, I am terrified at the prospect of leaving the house and working, however I will respect fathers wishes. Rupp my brother, I look forward to your home coming and hope that it is not toollong to wait,

Your loving sister,

Meena.

Kathmandu outside the hospital
chapter 13

Rajan Parayan, was hanging about, outside the dialysis unit of the Queen Elizabeth hospital in Kathmandu smoking non stop, while on the lookout for prospective clients,

When a Toyota 4x4 land cruiser pulled up, the driver got out went to the rear of the vehicle opened the doors operated the lever and the figure of a man sitting in a wheelchair appeared wearing sunglasses and baseball type hat with "I love NY", he immediately recognised the figure as that of Binod Chaudry, the wealthy carpet manufacturer from Jorpati for whom he had once worked for some years ago before he found an easier way of earning money,

Binods face looking more yellowish than tanned; the once portly figure now reduced to a mere skeleton, the loss of weight, and sallow complexion a sure sign of kidney problems, the result of a life of excessive alcohol abuse After a brief exchanged of pleasantries Rajan enquired,(as if he was concerned) at the state of his health. Binod explained that this was his bi-weekly visit to the unit for treatment for his failing kidneys

Rajan suggested that he could possibly help him as he understood his predicament as his sister had died a few years earlier from the same illness because she could not afford a transplant, At this statement Binod seemed to be interested, go on, what are you saying, you can help! yes sir I can! but this is neither the place nor time, for such a discussion, can I come to your home to-morrow and I will explain further, Binod instructed the driver to give Rajan his address and a time when he could come to the house to explain what he was offering, until to-morrow. Rajan scurried off to a local restaurant where he was known to the proprietor to celebrate his new contact with cup of strong coffee

Rajan Parayan, was a kidney racketeer who had previously served a jail term of three years in Nakkhu jail Kathmandu, convicted on a charge of selling more than 50 kidneys, a crime he was proud of! he was currently in the employ of the notorious Indian Surgeon Dr Amit Kumar, the most wanted doctor in India, Kumar had made millions from performing illegal transplants for those who could afford his services, he was not cheap not by a long chalk, But, when you are desperate to live and can afford to pay,money is no object especially for those who are desperate and hopefully Binod Chaudry was desperate.

Binod Chaudray lived in an palatial residence with ten bedrooms all with attached bathrooms a huge open plan living area where he entertained his clients, the house was littered with carpets from all over the world, from Kazakh rugs to Senneh, rugs from West Persia, carpets on the walls carpets on the floor, silk carpets wool carpets, carpets were once his passion., now he moved around the house restricted to a wheelchair unable to do any thing physical as the effort tired him quickly. The house was in the Teku district of the city near the Ram sith Temple, overlooking the river Bagmat Rika, .a house with beautiful views

Rajan was welcomed by the driver whom he recognised from the day before, shown directly into the living area where he was offered a seat.Tea! But he refused as he was anxious to get on with the business at hand, Chaudry soon appeared in his chair,acknowledged him with the normal pleasantries that is bestowed on visitors. and immediately asked Rajan to elaborate on the statement of yesterday. Rajan explained his relationship with Dr Amit Kumar, the well known kidney transplant specialist from Mumbai, how they could arrange for him to visit Dr Kumar's private clinic,in Mumba.

At the clinic he would receive a complete medical examination and some more tests, after which he would undergo a surgical operation to remove one of his now diseased kidneys and replace it with a healthy one, which would give him a new lease of life, He went on to explain that they had ready and willing donors who would gladly donate a kidney, but at a price.

Binod summoned tea to be served, and while this was carried out, pondered the offer for a few minutes. How much is this going to cost me? Shree, the cost to you would be the modest amount of Nepalese rupee 3,000,000.00 approx ($50,000) 50% deposit for on going expenses such as travel arrangements, hospitalisation , donor payment and the remaining 50% on completion and a satisfactory release from the clinic, we can supply you with names, addresses and telephone numbers for you to check of satisfied clients who have used our services in the past, prominent individuals that you may recognise for you to confer with before committing yourself to our arrangement .Let me think over your proposal for a few days, as it is a large amount of money. Leave your contact number, and l will be in touch,with that Rajan stood up and asked to be excused.

With business concluded be left Rajan was so confident that he had acquired a new client, that he ran, jumped and punched the air with his fist shouting yes! Releasing his pent up excitement!,

Now all I have to do was to visit Jorpati, the carpet manufacturing area of the city to seek out potential willing donors, who, for an attractive sum of money or a false promise of fame and fortune in India would give up one of their precious kidneys for just such an opportunity. And there were many takers as he knew all to well

Meeting with Parayan chapter 14

Over a period of time under Jothi, s direction, Meena became skilled at knotting,weaving and carding all the skills needed in the manufacture of carpets and rugs she also enjoyed the new found friendship of Jothi ,Jothi being a few years older, two to be exact,she introduced Meena to the way of life in the big city, the place where she was born and raised the coffee shops and restaurants that she frequented as their food was the best! They often went out in the evenings after work to the local restaurants where they would enjoy a hot curry and coffee, they would talk for hours about the Bollywood heart throbs such as , Shah Rukh Khan, Ainir Khan and Shahid kapoor their films, their life style what it must be like to be a movie star? the type of men they would hoped to meet and marry one day, music, television soaps, the list was endless.Meena told Jothi all about her family,her mum and dad but especially about her brother Rupp, her tall good hearted brother, who had joined the British army, she hoped that one day she would have the opportunity of introducing her to him when be came home on leave,hopefiuly in a few months time, according to his last letter his training was proceeding well and that they should complete their tour of duty   in less than a month,"the letter was already a month old.",

It was on one of these evening jaunts to the coffee shop for a Dhal Bhat talcurry that Meena and Jothi became acquainted with Rajan Parayan, the Nepalese representative of Bollywood ,so he said; he was in Kathmandu, on a current assignment on the lookout for new faces for the Indian film industry. He showed a keen interest in both girls, but more, much more so,in Meena and said on a number of occasions that she had the face of an angle and the figure of a film star, this made her feel shy as she had never been told such niceties before not even by her mother or brother, it made her face flush up red ,at the same time making her feel good inside, a feeling she had not experienced before, so when ever Rajan appeared at the coffee shop, when they were there enjoying a coffee and a curry, they were glad to see their new found friend ,he knew all the big stars and could talk for hours on the subject of Bollywood ,He like most Asian people had gained his knowledge from the bootlegged copies of popular videos which he had purchased from the street vendors, what he didn't know he would make up!

At their last meeting in the coffee shop he had suggested to the girls that he could arrange a meeting with a movie mogul in Mumbai, (Bombay), possible screen tests, and probably a contract, at first the girls thought that the was joking, and paid no attention to his statement until 'when he said all travelling and hotel expenses would be paid for, plus some spending money in Mumbai, the youngsters were suddenly all ears, "what an opportunity" if it were genuine! thought the girls

The girls said that they bad to discuss the proposal with their relatives and to get their approval for such an adventure, Rajan assured them that if necessary he could give them (their respective families) any assurances they would require of him if it would help them to attain approval. Jothi,s approval was almost instantaneous, but Meena, said that she had to wait until the weekend to consult her parents, however she felt confident that they would approve

Initially, Meenas father was totally against any proposal of her going off to Mumbai on a wild goose chase, as he put it but the more Meena kept up her relentless argument for the trip ,and the opportunity that it might bring the family, his opposition became less and less until finally he consented but with conditions,firstly, we will need to know where you are going and secondly which hotel you will be staying at,and if for any reason the trip does not mature as planned you must contact us immediately by telephone,Meena agreed to the conditions.Sunday evening could not come fast enough as Meena was desperate to see Jothi and inform her that she two would be going to Mumbai and to confirm her acceptance to Rajan on their next meeting at the coffee shop.

Monday went by at a snails pace and the end of the working day could not come quickly enough for the girls ,as soon as work finished for the day both girls showered changed and ran all the way to their favourite coffee shop for the usual treat of Bhat and coffee ,both hoping that Rajan was there when they arrived ,he wasn't they felt a little deflated but ordered the usual ,all the time looking towards the door ,hoping that he would appear.

Rajan was standing across the street from the coffee shop slightly out of view of anyone entering or leaving the premises as he did not want to be seen, he bad been there for some time, this was noticeable by the number of cigarettes stubs lying on the ground, he smoked incessantly a sure sign of someone who lived on their nerves!

He saw the girls running up the street and entering the coffee shop, by the way they were running they were in a hurry, a sure sign that they were excited. He settled himself smoked a few more cigarettes, tidied himself, crossed the road, entered the coffee shop as casual as you like, saw the girls tucking into their curries, he made a beeline for them 'they saw him coming and beckoned him over. The girls were in a rush. to tell him the good news they were talking together, trying to get as much out in the shortest possible time, girls, girls please! One at a time! A short pause settled themselves and confirmed that their respective families had given their consent for the trip to Mumbai. That is excellent news! Let us celebrate our good fortune by allowing me pay for your meal, they chatted for a time about all the things they would do on their visit to the city, especially shopping, a visit to the beach, they had never seen the ocean before at this point Rajan asked to be excused, he explained that it would take a few days to make all the arrangements for the journey and that he would give them notice as to when they could commence their journey to Mumbai. He told them to be at the coffee shop on Wednesday evening for final arrangements

On Wednesday evening after work the girls made their way as usual to the coffee shop where Rajan was waiting for them when they arrived, after the normal pleasantries, he explained that he had arranged for them both to fly out on Monday on Kingfisher flight KB 001 from Kathmandu to Mumbai direct,on arrival at the airport take a taxi to the YMCA, 18 YMCA road, Mumbai which is close to the Mumbai central bus depot in Kamathipura, the taxi will know where to take you!,I have booked a double room in Meenas name, you will both have to become temporary members of the YMCA, he then handed Meena 10,000 rps for the hotel and membership fees which have to be paid in advance and the left over money for them to spend on themselves in Mumbai for a few days until he arrives business complete they all talked about the great adventure that they were about embark upon

The following day the girls approached their employer and relayed their opportunity to him reluctantly very reluctantly he said that he would allow them a week off unpaid and that if they failed to return after that period their jobs would no longer exist and that they would be unemployed .the girls agreed

End of tour, the village chapter 15

Our tour of duty was coming to a close when reports started to filter through that a group of Taliban fighters had invaded a village in our sector, the gunmen were holding the village headman, his wife and two daughters to ransom under the threat of death, unless they helped the Taliban cause.

Sergeant Gunung, said that the people of the village needed our help and that it was our duty to go to their aid. We set out as usual after breakfast, our moral was high and our outlook even higher as a group there is nothing better than action that's why we joined the army ,for action and adventure, there is nothing but nothing like the real thing, you were full of excitement your thoughts and actions are quicker and faster and than normal and as the adrenalin pumps through your body you feel more alive that you have ever felt in your life, your are capable of the most super human tasks that presents themselves in that state of mind, I realise why people take drugs if this is the feeling of euphoria it gives you but we had clear heads for the task that we had embarked upon and knew what was required of us and we knew what our capabilities were. We arrived at the hill overlooking the village Captain Keith called up HQ we have arrived at map reference alpha gamma 225 and are surveying the position as instructed will inform as developments occur over. The captain advised that he needed a few volunteers to scout closer when it gets dark in order to ascertain the strength of the enemy in the village, everyone volunteered, sergeant Gunung chose four of the group and advised them, "do not at all cost make contact with the enemy"!, they were simply to observe and report back with their findings, be back here in two hours for debriefing, yes sir!, with that, they slipped off into the darkness in different directions towards the village The time past quickly while we were waiting, we checked and double checked our equipment just to keep busy, The scouts returned one by one and volunteered their information to the captain after assimilating all the facts he decided on a plan of action. Apparently the head man and his family were being held in the last house in the village, they were being guarded by two guards inside and four outside the house, they also had four guards at both ends of the village four Toyota pickup trucks two with a light machine guns mounted at the rear and an assortment of shoulder launched missiles all in all a well equipped small force.

Gather round, this is the situation, he outlined on the ground a drawing of the village the positions of the vehicles and the groups of defenders, we have the advantage, we have night vision goggles and that means that we can get into position as close to the target as is possible call up air support to take out the Toyota's. with the mounted machine guns leaving us to deal with the defenders at both ends of the village simultaneously while the captain, sergeant Gunung, and a squad which included my self hit the house front and back all to be coordinated with the air strike, the markers were designated their respective targets which they will mark with laser beams for a surgical strike, any questions, everyone clear on their assigned targets Yes sir!, was the reply,

The captain called up the air strike ,coordinates given estimated time of asset arrival ,watches, set orders to quietly move out, and a" final good hunting men", the scene set, we were as quiet as mice as we moved stealthily towards our designated positions once we reached our asigned targets, we squatted and observed over the situation, everything was quiet with little to no movement around the village ,we waited for the over head roar of a jet .The waiting was like an eternity. I looked up and saw the jet hurtling across the sky two streaks of vapour trails leaving from under each wing,a few moments later the explosions of the Toyota,s being obliterated the passengers unaware of what had hit them seconds latter the clatter of gun fire the units attacking their respective targets as we entered the building at breakneck speed the guards were surprised and confused and dealt with quickly without stopping we hit the windows and doors simultaneously the captain, tripped stumbled then fell headlong through the door. a bandit pounced on him knife in hand ,about to stab him in the back but before he could strike I shot him twice in the head as he fell I kicked the body out of the way ran to the room door kicked it open sergeant Gunning was first through he let off a couple of volleys, cried all clear the other rooms were cleared at the same break neck speed the headman and his family were all sitting on the floor, the girls crying the father trying to console them, the family safe, the house cleared we returned outside, an engine roared into life as the remnants of the Taliban intruders fled the scene.

Captain Keith, accosted me and thanked me for my action, but I was too pumped up to understand what he meant I was just doing what was required of me sir, and I am grateful for your action Chandra.

The village checked, the bodies counted, no casualties on our side we did a good job that's what soldering is all about", I thought!

The headman of the village thanked us repeatedly and offered us tea we thanked him but we had to secure the village before we could relax, we stayed until morning, and at first light, we did a perimeter sweep of the village searching for underground tunnels and the possibility of wounded Taliban fighters who might have tried to crawl of in the night. All clear was the result! The village is clear a promise of Afghani troops to visit and determine what could be done to protect the village against any further attacks and to help rebuild the small mosque an essential part of the everyday existence of the village in this hostile part of the world. "Job well done we returned to base with a feeling of satisfaction".

Rajans result chapter 16

It was a week later when the phone call came through, and as expected it was positive. Rajan, bad been working hard with a few prospective donors, and now that the prospect had turned into a reality he had to go and collect the deposit from Binod, supply him with references as requested, a telephone call to Dr. Kumar, to request a date when be can fit the new patient into his busy schedule .he loved it when things started to gel!

He had made his pitch to his prospective donors, one quickly accepted, one more approval and it would be a confirmed project, but he would have to wait a few days more.

Deposit received he set about booking the air tickets, and arranging the

Accommodations in Mumbai for both the recipient and prospective donors a straight forward duty, something be had done many times before. Dr. Kumar supplied Rajan with a schedule and the address of the new clinic where the kidney swap operations would be carried out.

With both donors confirmed and the schedule of arrangements complete Rajan had one more chore, a visit to Binod Chaudry, to give him his air tickets and travel arrangements. The arrangements were straight forward, He Rajan would accompany Binod on a Royal Nepalese flight from Kathmandu international to the Chattrabbi Shivaji airport in Mumbai on the following Tuesday, after Binods visit to the dialysis unit at the Queen Elizabeth hospital in Kathrnandu, a taxi ride from the Mumbai airport to the Chateau Windsor hotel at church gate on the Veer Nairman road, rest then a visit to Dr Kumar's clinic for a complete medical examination the following day prior to the kidney swap

The first thing Rajan did on his arrival in Mumbal was to call the YMCA to establish that the girls had arrived and that they were settled in their accommodation and to fix in his mind that his plans were still on track, a second call to Dr Kumar's clinic to confirm their arrival, and to confirm with the doctor, that everything was set for Binod to be brought to the clinic on Wednesday, for the examination and the eventual kidney swap the following day.

Early on Wednesday morning after breakfast of tea scrambled egg with toast Rajan arranged with Dr Kumar to send a vehicle to collect himself and Binaud to take them to the clinic .The vehicle duly arrived and transported them including his wheel chair to the clinic where they were welcomed by a young man who was waiting to transport Binaud to the doctors examination room all this time Binaud was quiet but his meeting with Dr Kumar he had many questions .how long will be here and how long will the operation take .The doctor informed and reassured him that the operation would take place tomorrow ,Thursday, after a good rest and preparation ,all co-ordinated with the arrival of the new kidney that was being donated the operation which he had carried out many times before would be straight forward and that after a few days with specialised care be would feel stronger, and be able to get up and that after that he would probably start to become more mobile and after a few more days he could probably fly back home without the wheelchair ,he pointed to the many chairs that were lined up in the hallway on his way into the surgery, the result of many successful operations!, the statement was aimed to build confidence in Binauds mind,after the examination was over the patient was wheeled of to a private room where he could relax and prepare himself for his coming operation

Dr. Kumar called Rajan into his office to discuss the situation with the donor Rajan confided that he had in fact brought two donors they are friends, and if I had only invited one I think they would not have come at all and that he would be entertaining them both at the "Great Khyber Pass restaurant", for a meal this evening, and that with the doctors assistance he would have his donors to-night in plenty of time for to-morrows exchange, Good!, unless I hear from you to the contrary, 1 will make the final preparations for to-morrow following a successful outcome of this evenings venture ",1 will be expecting your call!".

Rajan returned to the hotel to further his arrangements for the evening with his prospects. All bookings made be rested and contemplated his next move. He was happy that his part in the operation was almost over and that everything had so far gone without any problems.

Returning to England chapter 17

It was a week later that we would be returning to England during that week I received notice that for my actions at the village I was being promoted to sergeant "I was delighted", sgt Gunung and corporal Magarabedi said that I deserved the promotion for my quick thinking, I thought anyone of my comrades would have done the same, but as they pointed out, "you did it". And that's what counts. Within a few days we were airlifted back to RAF Brize Norton in Oxfordshire, then by bus to Catterick, it was like coming home. We were given a few days leave before being notified of further postings a team had been chosen under the command of Cpt. Keith and sgt, Gunung to return to Kathmandu to assisting helping with the new intake of recruits, I was excited that I had been chosen and my friend Magarabadi had also been chosen we were both happy, it meant that we could be with our families for a while, the others were posted to Belize, Brunei and Iraq. But a short rest first," we deserved it"!.

We joined the rest of the induction team on the flight back to Nepal, the captain told me that he was looking forward to seeing the country that he had heard so much about and that he looked forward to an authentic dhal curry

The flight back home gave me a few hours to reflect on the last fifteen months of my life, of how I started out as a youth determined to join the army, at all cost, and at just how green I was, a shy lad with little or no experience of the world outside Nepal, only what my father had told us, about his experiences in other countries, and his time with the British forces and how he had enjoyed the adventures and now I had followed in his foot steps and how proud of his son he was to followed in his foot steps to have been trained as a soldier and to have fought in a couple of battles and how the boy that I was, when I left ,was now a man and "all in the blink of an eye". I now knew why he felt the way he did,

I was looking forward to seeing my father, mother and especially my younger sister on my return.

Meena, who had written to me a few weeks ago, the letter although nice did not bode well with me, and I had a strange feeling that for some reason or other would not go away. Magarabedi said that he too was looking forward to a reunion with his family especially his older brother whom he told me was in the police, and that maybe he too! One day would like to join, but he was enjoying being a soldier, and all that goes with soldering in the British army

Fasten your seat belts please came the attendants voice, ladies and gentlemen we will be landing at Kathmandu International airport, in a few minutes came the voice the temperature will be 28 degrees centigrade with clear skies, thank you! For flying with Nepalese airways, and we hope to see you again the plane suddenly shook as the wheels touched down on the tarmac of the runway, the rest of the passengers on board started to applaud.

Dr Kumar and the clinic chapter 18

Dr Kumar's clinic was situated on the corner of Bhulubai Desai Marg, and Pantai road, the clinic was leased from the Nam Fatt family ,a well respected Chinese trading family who arrived in Mumbai at the end of the 19th century, brought in by the British to carry out work within the British army bases situated in (Bombay),Mumbai at that time, they remained after the British left and did well selling dry goods, fruits and rice, which the family still hold the concessions. The front of the clinic faced to-wards the sea and was ideal for those recuperating from a major operation as the tranquility of the sea coupled with the smell of ozone helped speed up the recuperation process.

Johnson and Johnson gardens were on the left of the building and on the same side was the gated entrance through which brought you into a court yard with buildings set out in a inverted L shape ahead was the main building and living quarters the long side being the clinic and operating theatre area parking for twenty or more cars all surrounded by high walls gave the clinic a look feel of privacy away from prying eyes.

The Truphati apartment block situated on the far right of the building overlooked the complex from a far and the Chung Fa, art gallery was their nearest neighbour across the road.a pair of dragons graced the entrance painted in red and gold typical of chinese culture

The clinic was chosen carefully and strategically by Dr. Kumar, as the Parsi general and the Jasiok hospital and research centres were only a stones throw away, this gave the Cumbala Hill clinic respectability as it was well situated in an area which abounded with healing centres.

Dr Kumar was the son of a wealthy Indian industrialist, his father sponsored him during his studies to attain his Doctorate in England, he worked for a number of years at the London City General where he gained a reputation among his peers as a young man with the gift for healing, "his private life was something else", he returned to India after a scandal involving a high class call girl and blackmail, it was also rumoured that he was moonlighting, but never proven carrying out abortions for the rich and wealthy, people who paid well for his services and silence, and wanted their reputations and identities kept secret.

Dr.Kumar's father paid a lot of money to cover up the family shame.ordering his son to return to India! Dr Kumar loved the high life, gambling and woman were his passion but be was unlucky in love and even unluckier in gambling, losing was something he regulary experienced, but he was a magnificently skilled surgeon, an artist when it came to surgery in that, "he was brilliant," in a class of his own, and he knew it, his illegal operations paid for his love of women and roulette.

On returning to Asia he teamed up with an old friend Sita Gupta, who was well connected in high places, they formed a partnership and a thriving business in Prostitution and kidney transplants

Dr Kumar, employed a number of agents throughout the Indian sub continent whose sole purposes was to keep him supplied with wealthy clients requiring immediate life and death surgery ,out with the normal channels and kidney transplants were a lucrative business. Clients and donors alike were plentiful in the sub continent, but illegal ,hence his extortionate fees. He had just released a grateful client, and was preparing for his next operation on one Binod Chaudry from Nepal who had been brought to him by his trusted employee, Rajan Parayan, they had completed fifty or more successful operations over the years and although Rajan had spent a term in jail selling kidneys he did not divulge his employers name, Dr Kumar, showed great generosity towards Rajan for such loyalty. He was currently awaiting a call from Rajan who was arranging for him two prospective kidney donors for the new client.

Mumbai chapter 19

The flight from Kathmandu to Mumbai was very uneventful except for this being their first flight they were very nervous about flying but they soon settled into flight once the plane had taken off, after lift of they began to relax and enjoy the view from out the window which in turn made them forget all their worries about flying? The rest of the flight they either slept or looked at the magazine or visiting the rear toilet~

The taxi journey from the airport would have been purely a site-seeing venture except the driver kept asking all sorts of questions like ,where did they come from,! What were they doing here? question after question. They told him, that they were here at the kind benevolence of the Bollywood representative in Kathmandu shree man Rajan Parayan, who had promised to show them the city lights and to arrange meetings with the movie moguls and the possibility of screen tests and maybe even a contract. The driver had heard it all before, wished them good luck, after advising them not to build their hopes too high! As many a dream had been shattered by young hopeful actresses looking to make it big in Bollywood.

The girls arrived at the YMCA, paid the driver, thanked him for his advice and went straight to the reception desk, a young man courteously asked if he could be of service to them, They explained that a double room had been booked in the name of Meena Chandra, and as they were not members of the YMCA that they would like also to have a temporary membership for three months, He checked his register and nodded approval to Meena, would you please fill in these forms with your names date of birth and place of birth etc,the girls obliged ,paid the required monies and were then shown to their room by a young boy dressed in a military uniform ,he opened the door, ushered them in then gave the key to Meena and said that he hoped that they enjoyed their stay at the YMCA,the room was spacious with a central double bed a telephone table and phone at the side a double wardrobe facing the bed a hand basin in one corner and a two seater wicker settee for them to sit on all decked out in white which gave the room a feeling of space the window directly opposite the settee was open and the smells from the city as well as the heat came wafting into the room The girls thought that this was just heaven, they put their belongings in the wardrobe, sat on the bed and discussed where they would go first, the beach, cinema or shopping, the decision was arrived unanimously "shopping!" But first things first call our families to let them know that we have arrived safely and to give them a contact number here in Mumbai, in case of emergencies as promised, a short nap, a shower, then a short outing to find out the best shopping in the city.

The receptionist advised them to exit the building and turn left and just walk we are only minutes away from the main shopping in Kamathipura ,there were restaurants galore accessories shops, shops selling mobile phones, shops selling sweets the smells the vibrancy of a bustling ,busy area the like they had never experienced before even in Kathmandu, it only took the girls minutes to discover the first magical shop selling saris ,in fact they could not mistake the shop,saris,head scarves and printed material hung down from the lines which stretched across the shop front and music blared out the latest hit song of the latest bollywood blockbuster at the time "kuch kuch hota hai", with Sharuk Khan .They entered holding each other by the arm and giggling with excitement at the sight of the many differing patterns styles and colours ,and the noise the like they had never seen or heard before,a virtual Aladdin's cave and they loved it! Even more interesting was the big notice in the window which stated in big bold letters up to 70% discount on selected items they rummaged through all the offers, until finally, settled on the colour and style of their chosen saris Meena chose orange colour with a gold paisley pattern running through it, a pair of flip flops orange with gold and silver circles around the toe grip, matching silver combs for her long black hair and a hand bag, something that she had always longed for but could never afford

Jothi, on the other hand chose a lime green sari with a traditional silver embroidered Bengali motif running through it matching bangles, similar flip flops to Meena and a hand bag, they felt like royalty! After paying for their treasures the next stop a visit to a restaurant for a meal. "Bombay duck "was the order of the day, they had heard so much about this specialty food from Mumbai that they just wanted to try the taste for themselves.

They didn't take long to choose a place to eat, in fact they were spoilt for choice, however, they chose the "Tadj Mahal restaurant" because of its connotations with love and romance, they entered the restaurant and made a beeline for a table just in front of the window so they could continue watching the wonders of the city as they ate.

The waiter arrived note book in hand and politely asked what was their desire, "Bombay duck", they retorted in unison,and so you shall, said the waiter ,and a drink while you wait for your food ,water please,a pitcher of cool water soon arrived with two glasses a second waiter much, much younger than the first also came to the table with banana leaves which he spread out ,one each, next came the waiter with sweat pickles

Dahl ,mint and other savouries which he proceeded to place on their respective leaves,"looks good so far said Meena"!, the main dish arrived placed before them with the words enjoy! Jothi took the first hand full put it in her mouth looked at Meena and said its fish! a moment of silence followed by a roar of laughter ,the waiter rushed over to ascertain the situation, "We were expecting duck", Ah yes!, Bombay duck is in fact fish. They drank their water ate their meal which they thoroughly enjoyed, talking all the time about their adventure so far Jothi felt a little foolish at not knowing about the meal but they were having a good time and that's what matters. They sat in the restaurant talking what seemed like an eternity until Jothi intimated that she was now beginning to feel tired and suggested they return to the YMCA and get some sleep.

As they made their way back to their room with their new clothes they decided that to-morrow they would visit the famous beach at Chow patty and spend the day there. They both showered in the YMCA hall shower located on their floor, back in the room they talked quietly, but it faded away as tiredness caught up with them. Both were asleep in seconds

Monday morning both girls were up at first light showered combed their long hair to untangle it put on their new saris admired themselves in the wardrobe mirror went down stairs and asked the reception the best way to go to. Chowpatty beach The receptionist advised that they took a short stroll to the central bus station which was just within walking distance of the where they were a number 24 bus at stand 5 will take you to marine drive terminus from there you can walk the full length of the beach, he further explained that the beach is quiet in the daytime and only came to life at night .We just want to see the ocean as we have never seen the sea .They thanked him for his advice and wandered off to the bus station .The bus station was very busy, buses coming and buses going ,they managed to locate stand five and boarded the bus to the beach. they sat on the lower deck of the bus and watched and chatted all the way to the shore ,they alighted the bus at the terminus and walked across the road to the beach, the beach was a mixture of sand and pebbles, no trees or bushes for shade but clean such a clean beach for one so popular, immediately they removed their flip flops and ran to the waters edge dipped their toe in the water and kicked water on each other laughing and screaming and enjoying the experience of the sea something to tell their families, after a time they returned to the road away from the beach, they were both hungry in all excitement of the adventure they had forgotten all about food, a child was sitting under the shade of a canopy which was the shelter for a small vending business the child had his legs bent totally under his body, he looked as though he had not eaten for a week as he looked so emaciated and thin, an old tin by his side his outstretched arms asking for alms pulled at Meenas heart strings, without hesitation she opened her new bag took out some money and placed it in the tin ,buy something nice to eat young man she said with a tear in her eye as she too had experience hunger.

Sadness hit the girls at the thought of the boy ,but he was one of many poor in this large city, as they walked on a little they were much quieter due to the presence of the little boy bringing home to them the other side of Mumbai. Gupta's bhel puri stall loomed up in front of them and quickly dispersed their gloomy thoughts, hunger was gnawing at their insides as they decided to have one, two please!said Meena to the stall holder ,bhel pun salads are crisp puffed rice and semolina doused in chutney and scooped up in a flat fried pun

69

one of the specialties of Chow patty beach ,as they ate they crossed the street out of the sun and came directly to a fortune teller who told Meena that she had a lucky face ,cross my palm with silver and I will tell your fortune excited at the prospect the girls sat down opposite the soothsayer, Meena first gave 10 rupees held out her hands ,palms up, and listened :you have traveled a long way ,you have worked hard all your young life ,and suffered many hardships, I see travels to foreign lands ,you will be prosperous in your life and so on and so on. Jothi handed over her 10 rupees , the fortune teller warned her of future trouble and to be careful of strangers who will want to take from her but mostly the nice things that you expect of fortune tellers both were told of their happy marriages and the number of children they would have ,both girls satisfied they wandered on. A juggler on a bike asked for money, they duly offered 10 rupees ,and he duly entertained them with a spectacular juggling and balancing act the like they had never seen before juggling balls juggling hoops while riding a monoped a (bicycle with one wheel)it was just like magic to the girls ,a wonderful day they were having in each others company .Meena turned to Jothi and said :no matter what happens in the future Jothi, I hope we remain friends for the rest of our lives and that the past few days have been unforgettable, Jothi agreed ,and they walked back to the bus terminus hand in hand feeling happy to be in each others company .

They returned to their room still holding hands and going over and over their adventures so far ,a quick meal, nap and a shower and a visit in the evening to the cinema to see the latest Bollywood blockbuster Kuch Kuch Hota Hai staring Shahruk Khan.

On Tuesday morning the girls breakfasted in the YMCA dining room they ate rice, fish and scrambled egg washed down with a cup of Indian tea, after which they returned to their room, as they opened the door to the room the telephone rang, Jothi answered, it was the voice Rajan Parayan, he said,that he would be arriving in Mumbai later to-day, he would be busy arranging interviews for them and that he would be unable to meet with them until Wednesday evening, where upon be would entertain them to a meal, at a very special restaurant, he enquired to their financial status!, we have plenty of money sir, said Jothi! If everything is well with you, I will call in person at the YMCA, to-morrow around seven o'clock collect you both, and to bring you up to date with my arrangements, see you soon !with that he rang off.

The girls decided that they would pay a visit to Crawford market to buy presents for their families, Meena, suggested that they went by the old taxis that they noticed the other day while travelling on the bus ,they were reminiscent of the old 50,s fiats that were very popular, they were informed by the receptionist. On Monday they were trying to cram as much into their holiday before they returned back to the factory ,although in the back of their minds they hoped secretly that something nice would emanate from Mr Parayans meetings with the Bollywood moguls ,but for now they just wanted to do as much as possible .The market was a bustling place of fruit stalls ,bag stalls ,Indian Knick sknack stalls, soapstone elephant stalls all shrouded in the loud barking of traders offering their bargains to anyone that ventured close to their stalls.

Mumbai chapter 19

The girls wondered around examining the material at an Indian fabric stalls, this would be nice for my mum ,said Meena,! Look at that sari that would look good on my sister, its her colour and that's how they carried on at every stall they visited they were enjoying themselves and forgot all about the time .They found a small tea shop, entered and ordered some tea, curry puffs and rice cakes, as they ate they talked about their purchases and about what to do on Wednesday to keep themselves busy before their meeting in the evening with Rajan Pariyan. I know, said Jothi,! We'll go to the museum! "A good idea" said Meena,decision made they made their way to the entrance of the market where the old taxi's were waiting for fares ,they asked the first in line to take them back to the YMCA where a shower and more talk on what to wear tomorrow on their dinner date. a whole discussion followed before they fell sleep happy in the knowledge that they had purchased gifts for their families from Mumbai.

After breakfast the following morning, the girls asked the best way to get to the Chhatrapati Shivaji Maharaj Vastu Sangrahalaya (the prince of Wales museum)so called after the visit of the Prince of Wales who later became King George the second .they were advised to take a taxi to Mahatma Ghandi road ,which they duly did. The taxi arrived in front of the building which stood proud in the mist of beautiful lush gardens edged with palm trees they paid the driver and made their way into the museum itself paid the entrance fee and entered the world of the Gupta Empire 280- 550 ad ,ancient Indian articles of Gupta script the script used for writing Sanskrit during the Gupta Empire,then on through Islamic Sultanates 1206-1596 ,onward to the

Mogul Empires 1526-1707 and finally to the British India 1858-1947 onward through the terrible weaponry of the various empires. they visited the natural history section which disappointed them as the exhibits were in a very scruffy and dusty condition but it was a museum and exhibits get like this as they stand behind their glass protection. They were in awe at the Ahimsa exhibition ,of the statues of Bahubali and the meaning behind the cult ,they found a statue of Thangkas the Buddhist who originated from Nepal ,all in all an engrossing day, which went too quickly Meena shook Jothi,s arm to let her know that it was time to return to the YMCA, to shower and to prepare for the treat promised by Rajan, They had another enjoyable day ,although much quieter and more serious than the days before ,but still enjoyable ,in its own way.

They left the museum found a taxi and returned to their room, they took turns at showering and were soon looking their best for their expected visitor They did not have to wait long, they had just sat down to plan when the phone rang, It was the reception informing them that they had a visitor in reception and could they come down.

The evening meal chapter 20

Rajan Parayan arrived at the YMCA at around seven fifteen and immediately told the receptionist that he had come to collect Miss Meena and Miss Jothi, the receptionist called their room and informed them that they had a guest .The girls arrived about ten minutes later .They greeted each other with a hands clasped and a short bow,followed by a brief hug ,like old friends .

I have booked a table at" The Khyber Pass sea food restaurant",the booking is for eight thirty They exited the YMCA and took a taxi directly to the restaurant, Rajan told them that he had been busy arranging meetings for them with very important film makers and that they were looking forward to meeting the girls, They arrived at the Restaurant entered ,and were greeted by a turbaned usher who enquired if they had a booking,Rajan confirmed that he booked a table earlier, Ah, yes sir!, Mr Rajan, we have been expecting you and your party, they were immediately directed to a table in a corner behind silk curtains, they were handed a menu each, and after a discussion decided on Shark fin soup followed by buttered prawns, crab, grouper in Soy sauce and a salad of fresh mixed vegetables, the meal ordered a jug of water and a beer for Rajan was also ordered That done the girls asked to be excused as they would like to visit the ladies room ,as they got up to leave the jug of water and two glasses arrived followed by a kingfisher beer for Rajan .The opportunity for Rajan to adulterate the water presented itself almost immediately, and he took the phial from his pocket unstoppered it and poured it into the jug with out anyone noticing .He took out a cigarette lit it ,and sat their puffing with a smug smile on his face .the girls returned,full of excitement and giggling, they were anxious to here what Rajan had to tell them ladies!, let me pour you a drink , thank you, they replied, and at that he carried out his task , as the girls sipped their water he told them that he had made an appointment with Ahamad Chatrabatti the famous Bollywood director, and on Saturday the following day a visit to the studios where they will be given a screen test .The soup arrived and was distributed by a waiter wearing white gloves, the soup went down well,and was followed by the buttered prawns which the girls enjoyed immensely ,a further few sips of water, then the crabs arrived, they had fun with the crabs, breaking the shell with a hammer and sucking the meat from the legs, a new experience for the pair ,a further drink of water then the fish and salad by now the conversation was on the film they saw on

Monday evening and their hope that the interview with the mogul would be successful

Rajan was smiling at the girls enthusiasm which was infectious and the more they talked the more they sipped their drinks , after a while Meena said that she had to go to the toilet ,she was not feeling well ,must be all that food you ate, said Rajan,! Jothi said that she would accompany her. At the toilet Jothi said she too, felt sharp pains in her stomach .Rajan Knew exactly what was happening as the girls vanished through the toilet door he took the opportunity to call Dr. Kumar, and asked him to instruct the driver to come to the

"Khyber pass sea food restaurant" .The girls emerged thirty minutes later looking very pale, they asked that they be taken back to the YMCA ,Of course replied Rajan, immediately !and at that he asked for the bill ,which he paid at the desk on the way out.

Outside, Jothi threw up, and instantly felt embarrassed at such an act, after all that good food, Meena, followed suit, Rajan showed alarm, hailed the car which was down the road a little and suggested that he took them to a doctor to have them checked out.

Oh thank you!, thank you!,Rajan they both echoed , they stepped into the car and the car sped off ,at break neck speed Rajan told the driver to go to the Cumbala Hill Clinic as fast as he could .Rajan said "that he felt fine!, and it must have been the water that they drank, as he drank only beer,

They arrived at the clinic entered the court yard ,exited the car and again threw up almost immediately ,then cleaned themselves with a tissue from their handbags, as Rajan and the driver guided them into the doctors waiting room.

The evening meal chapter 20

They did not have to wait long; the doctor appeared almost immediately, he asked what was the matter? , he directed the question at Meena first, she said that she had abdominal pains and that she was bringing up her food, I also feel a little dizzy, Jothi concurred with Meenas statement he then instructed Jothi to go into his surgery go behind the screen and remove her sari down to the waist and lie down on the couch ,he followed ,and pressed around her stomach, tell me when it hurts, the doctor knew exactly where to press to get the maximum effect Jothi jumped, there! doctor just there, I will have to give you a sedative to relax you and some pills to neutralise the pain, you can rest in the clinic to-night with that he asked her to dress, handed her the pills with a glass of water and while she drank it down, gave her an injection, after a good nights rest you should feel fine young lady.

The driver was called and Jothi was conveyed to a private room. Meena was next. The doctor went through the same procedure and Meena was taken to a separate room from Jothi, Both girls sedated and kept apart so that the doctor could carry out the next part of his plan, the next phase would be carried out at first light to-morrow morning.

Dr. Kumar took Rajan back to his office and congratulated him on a well planned operation he indicated that he only required one kidney at this juncture but the tall girl, Meena, was a real beauty and that he had decided that he would give her to Sita ,to instruct her in the rudiments of entertaining men. That one! She can make plenty of money for us, on a regular basis, instead of just removing her kidney for a one off payment, I know of clients that can overly afford to pay for the services of such a beauty, a joint agreement was quickly acknowledged after which Dr. Kumar instructed Rajan to return to the hotel and wait for his instructions.

The following morning the operation commenced on time, Binaud Chaudry was prepped ,sedated and wheeled to the main operating theatre, Jothi,"the chosen one", was further sedated and prepped without regaining consciousness' from the evening before, she was conveyed to another smaller theatre for the removal of her vital organ,

Everything went like clockwork Binauds diseased kidney removed and replaced with Jothis healthy one" a good days work for the skilled surgeon and his specialist staff"!.

After the successful removal of Jothis kidney she was stitched up, bandaged and wheeled back to her room of the evening before. The driver was given instructions to inform Rajan to come and help him return her to her room at the YMCA, which he duly complied with, they wrapped her in a blanket and transported her back by their specially adapted van. At the YMCA, they carried her to the reception and informed the receptionist that she bad been drinking too much! the night before and that she needed plenty of rest and not to be disturbed ,they paid her bill for a few more days gave a sizable tip to the receptionist to keep the whole affair quiet for Jothis sake more that anything else ,they further explained that Meena her friend was attending an important interview and would probably return later in the evening .Everything covered they took her to the room placed Jothi on the bed covered her with a blanket and left. Remember! they advised the receptionist she needs plenty of quiet! Ensure she is not disturbed,and at that they left.

Back at the YMCA chapter 21

Jothi started to come around, and for a few moments did not recognise where she was but as the mist started to clear from her eyes she realised that she was back at the YMCA, how did I get here? Who brought me? How long have I been here? Questions, questions in her mind, she started to rise to get out of the bed, a sharp pain in her side stopped her, she moved her hand down to soothe the pain but instead she touched a soft moist bandage around her waist, she brought her had back to look at what was causing the wetness, blood, it was covered in blood. She shrieked, fear and fright griped her as she tried in her mind to work out what had happened, Meena! Meena! Where are you? I need you, help me I'm bleeding ,l,m bleeding,!! Meena I need help P L E A S E, Meena, but no reply just the noise and the bustle of the outside world going about its daily business, slowly, but slowly ,Jothi realised that she was alone and that Meena wasn't there Rajan Parayan,s promises were all false ,he was a kidney racketeer !he had sweet talked us into thinking that we were destined for Bollywood stardom ,and all the time he had planned to steal our kidneys. Her mind was in turmoil, Why me? Why me? I have been violated they have intruded into my body without my permission and stolen my kidney, I will die, oh! God, what has happened to me, why! Why! Why! Where is Meena Oh! Meena, please help me , she let out a scream the like she had never done before, the pain now starting to hurt more and more as the tears came rolling down her face like a waterfall .Nothing, but nothing made sense anymore ,through all her anguish and pain the phone kept ringing, — ring, ring, ring, ring, non stop ring, ring, she made a grab with her left hand managed to grip the mouth piece ,she held it tightly ,it came off the cradle, she brought it to her mouth and screamed "Help me"! "Help me", and at that she let go the phone and passed Out.

Meena started to came around, slowly at first ,then as her eyes cleared ,she immediately recognised the smell of jasmine and the subdued light that she was in a strange room, she sat up with a start ,but could only admire the decor the ceiling was awash in beautiful flowing silks which came together at a point in the centre around a bejeweled chandelier, the walls lined with pictures of naked woman in seductive poses , silks soft furnishings in pastel colours ,animal skins scattered on the floor, coupled with the rich aroma gave the room an air of seduction. As she tried to assimilate the ambiance of the room, the door opened and the face of a once beautiful woman appeared, your are awake?, how do you feel ,can I get you anything,

Where am I? , where is Jothi? How did I get here? And what am I doing here?, first things first. Both you and your friend were taken to doctor Kumar's clinic poisoned by something in the food you ate a few evenings ago, the doctor administered both of you with a sedative to help you sleep and something for the pain, unfortunately in the early hours of the morning your friend Jothi took a turn for the worst, doctor Kumar tried his utmost to save her but to no avail, and unfortunately your friend died!, what did you say? I said your friend Jothi she died, a few days ago, Dr. Kumar made arrangements with Mr. Rajan to escort her body back to Kathmandu, Meena started to cry she fell back into the bed and cried for a long time. When she eventually pulled herself together, the woman said that her name was Sita and that Dr. Kumar had asked her to care for her for a time. A knock at the door heralded the appearance of a young girl with a plate of rice and dhal curry and some japattis, and a glass of water, eat my dear you must be hungry, the tray of food was deposited at the foot of the bed and they both left, leaving her to her grief.

Meena tried to eat but the news of Jothis death shocked her so much that food was the last thing she wanted, she felt responsible, it was her, Meena, who brought her here to Mumbai, and now her best friend was dead ,the tears came again and she started sobbing deeply she lay her head on the pillow, brought her knees up to her chest, clasped her hands in prayer and prayed for forgiveness she cried and cried and eventually cried herself to sleep.

Return of the warrior chapter 22

I rushed through the front door as I had done many times before dropping my kit as I went, The first person to greet me was my mother, as soon as she saw me, she lunged at me with open arms shouting my name Rupp, Rupp its you its really you the tears of joy running down her face, next my father appeared with a broad grin wondering what was all the noise, Its Rupp Father ,Its our son Rupp he's come home and look at him so smart and so grown up and so soldierly more hugs and embraces and tears then when our emotions settled I asked where is Meena , Meena is in Mumbai, with her new friend Jothi, they have gone on an all paid visit, courtesy of the Bollywood representative Rajan Parayan,she called a few days ago and left a contact number where we could contact her in case of an emergency, "which this is" !,call her Rupp? She will be excited at hearing your voice, with that Rupp dialed the number the phone was answered by a male voice, good day this the Mumbai YMCA ,can I help you, can I speak to one of your guests Meena Chandra please ,one moment sir while I connect you with her room,

The phone rang for a while before being answered the voice cried help me! help me,! and then silence. Rupp was shocked who could it be what has happened it wasn't his sisters voice it must be her friend she sounds like she is in trouble, he re dialed the number again and asked the reception to send someone to the room to investigate as he felt sure that something terrible had happened to the occupants, please hurry I will call back in ten minutes.

After ten minutes had lapsed he again rang the number, sir the friend of your sister is in a terrible condition we do not know what has happened to her but she seems to be bleeding from her side, we have called the hospital and as soon as they arrive they will take her to the infirmary, we have not seen your sister today sir!.Give me your address, please, Rupp he wrote it down ,reserve a room for me I will be there as soon as I can arrange a flight to Mumbai, and at that he put the phone down, he explained the situation to his parents, I'm going to Mumbai on the first available flight ,don't worry mum, dad I'll find her the phone rang again this time it was Lance corporal Magararbedi, Rupp, I am going to Mumbai, my brother is working on a case there and may not be back for a time so I have decided to spend a few days with him and see Mumbai at the same time, Maga I am going there too, meet me at the airport and we will go together I will fill you in on the details when we meet, he put the phone down kissed his mother and shook his father by the hand, I will see you both in a few days time with Meena ,with that he left the house grabbed his gear and headed to get a bus back to the airport and to arrange a flight to Mumbai,.

At the airport Rupp met Maga his friend he explained the situation, how he called the YMCA to speak to his sister, how his sisters friend was found in bed with a bloody bandage around her waist, I suspect Rupp, said Maga, it sounds to me like someone has removed her kidney and dumped her in the YMCA my brother has told me that this kind of thing happens all the time, some people do it willingly for much needed money, while others do not. My brother can help you he is in Mumbai at the request of his superior and is familiar with this kind of affair,! I will call him and arrange for him to meet us at the YMCA on our arrival if it is convenient, Maga called his Brother with the view to meeting him at the YMCA, but his brother informed him that he was currently on a case and that it might be sometime before they can meet.

The travel agent was able to arrange a passage on an early flight to Mumbai, there was a cancellations on a flight out of Kathmandu international ,that same day, and if they hurried they should be able to catch the flight. They picked up their tickets and made their way to the airport checking in desk,made their reservation and then headed to the departure lounge where the could relax before the flight to Mumbai .Rupp told Magga what had happened on the phone to the YMCA , and it was imperative that he get there as quickly as possible,the passage passed at a gallop, before they new it they were being called for their flight,"thank goodness for that said Rupp" ,Relax Rupp, said Magga you cannot do anything until we reach Mumbai Magga called his brother to inform of his arrival itinery and his time of arrival ,His brother replied that should be at the Nair hospital around that time,He informed his brother that he should check into the YMCA and then make his way to the hospital."will do said Magga",I look forward to seeing you soon brother.

Rupp and Magga in Mumbai chapter 23

As soon as they arrived at the airport in Mumbai they took a taxi directly to the YMCA, there they were escorted to the managers office, where the manager informed them of the situation to date, as he understood it, Jothi Rama the girl who was sharing the room with Rupp's sister had been taken to the Nair Hospital, she was delivered here a few days ago by two male escorts ,who informed the reception that she had been drinking and that she should not be disturbed, however one of our room cleaning maids heard screaming from her room and called me to come up to investigate, when we entered the room we found the young lady in question lying halfway out of the bed with heavily soiled blooded bandages around her waist ,we realised what had happened to the young girl and immediately called the hospital and I assume they in turn notified the police.

Can we leave our luggage here, while we visit the hospital, of course sir!, said the manager. Please stay here at the YMCA at our pleasure until you have completed your business in Mumbai . With that he rang a bell, and a youth appeared, take their luggage to the presidential rooms,Both Rupp and Magga thanked the manager and then accompanied the porter to the presidential suite,their luggage deposited a key received and a card with the address ,they then proceeded out of the rooms to the entrance,past the reception where they found a taxi to take them to the Nair Hospital, which was situated on Malana Azad road south.

They arrived at the hospital entrance and as they passed through the main doors they were met by Detective Magarabedi, who quickly embraced his brother, they were in their own little world for a few moments when Maga broke free and said, brother! ,"this my friend corporal Chandra, or Rupp to his friends" ,how are you soldier?,I am known as Baburan,to my friends."I am pleased to make your acquaintance"; Any friend of Narayan is a friend of mine, let us sit over here for awhile so that I can tell you what we know, but first let me instruct the reception that I am here, and if there are any changes in the patient in room 19,s condition to inform me immediately.

They sat down, then he started, about a month ago, one Rajan Parayan was released from jail after serving a three year jail term for kidney trafficking, my superiors instructed me to follow and observe this person as I was familiar with all aspects of the case, they hoped that he eventually would lead us the whereabouts of one Dr. Amit Kumar, a once eminent surgeon now suspected of illegal kidney swap operations

The suspect made contact with one Binod Chaudry, at the QE2 kidney dialysis unit where he was under going his biweekly treatment and a further number of visits to his home, during this time he was visiting the Jorpati area of the capital meeting with two young women employed in the carpet industry, About ten days ago he purchased a number of air tickets to Mumbai, at a local travel agent, he purchased two business tickets to Mumbai one for himself and one for Binod Chaudry, two further budget tickets in the names of Jothi Rama, and Meena Chandra ,whom according to my younger brother Narayan, is your sister;yes, yes she is, Do you know where she is, at this point, enquired Rupp I'm afraid not! In cooperation with the local Mumbai police, we have been shadowing this Rajan Parayan, to date he has visited the Chateau Windsor Hotel, where we presume he was staying, the Cumbala Hill Clinic, the YMCA, and the "great Khyber Pass restaurant", accompanied by the two girls. I am hoping that when the young woman comes around she can identify a photograph of Parayan, and hopefully we can get a clearer picture of what is going on. Until that happens we just have to wait.

All three sat quietly in the main waiting area hoping that a nurse would appear and instruct them to follow her to the patient in room 19 Rupp and Narayan both dozed of for a while until a nurse was shaking them,"the doctor will see you now", the two stood up and made their way to where the doctor and Detective seargent Magarabedi were standing ,deep in conversation.

Jothi awakes chapter 24

Jothi, came around slowly at first, the pain of her last waking moments permeating slowly through to her mind, the room was different It wasn't the YMCA it was different and smelled different too!, she slipped her hand down to her side a numb pain but bearable and it felt dry, "I must have been dreaming before," She opened her eyes fully and scanned the room, I'm in a hospital!, I remember, Meena and I were sick, Rajan brought us to the clinic and the doctor examined me, he administered a sedative and gave me some pills," food poisoning ",he said ,now I'm back in the hospital thank god!, it was just a horrible dream. The door opened and a nurse appeared lifted her wrist and checked her pulse, I see you are awake!, you have had a terrible time, young lady ,the doctor will tell you what has happened to you, the nurse then pressed the button by the bed and then busied herself tidying the bed ,the doctor appeared with a stethoscope around his neck ,which he deployed to checked her heart rate "How are you feeling my dear"? , Jothi retorted I don't really know doctor I am confused, you are not the doctor who examined me last night, No Jothi am not, you have been here at the Nair General for two days and nights. Have I! Yes Jothi, you have, someone has removed one of your kidneys, whoever did this to you knew exactly what they were doing, the operation you have been through has been very professionally and skillfully carried out, "you are a very lucky young woman". Will I live doctor, of course you will, you are a perfectly healthy young woman, human beings have nearly two of everything and can still function normally when they lose the use of a part of their anatomy. in a day or two you will be feeling much stronger and a few days after that you should be walking around just like any normal person . Jothi!, the police are outside and would like to speak with you, that's if you are up to the task. Doctor where is

Meena. "I don't know Jothi" ,we collected you from the YMCA, that's all I can tell you, thank you doctor, I can face up to my predicament now that you have explained it to me. Please ask the police to come in, I will Jothi, and at that he vanished out through the door.

The doctor beckoned detective Sergeant Magarabedi over and told him that the girl Jothi, was awake, and that she was willing to talk to him, don't tire her too much .1 won't,! and at that he motioned the two soldiers over, they were then ushered into room 19, where Jothi was. Magarabedi introduced himself and explained why he was here in Mumbai, then introduced his brother Narayan and Rupp, Rupp is your friend Meena,s brother. Both these young soldiers have come here to find your friend, so, Jothi you can understand that we need you to tell us as much as you can remember, take your time ,if you feel tired we can go outside and let you rest. and come back later.

Jothi explained everything, going back to when they first encountered Rajan Pariyan in the coffee shop in Kathmandu, to when they went out to the "Great Khyber pass restaurant", to how she and Meena became sick and how Pariyan took them to a doctor who examined them and gave us both medicine and then sedated us, after that I recall waking up in our room at the YMCA for a brief while, then here. Sergeant Magarabedi produced a photograph of Pariyan and showed it to Jothi, Do you know this man! Yes I do, that is Rajan Pariyan, the so called Bollywood representative, so he told us, can you remember the doctors name, no sir, I was too sick at the time ,I just wanted the pain to go away, Thank you Jothi for all your help ,and at that they excused themselves and left her to sleep.

Detective sergeant Magarabedi, took his brother and Rupp back to the YMCA in a police car, on the way a call came on his hand phone, he listened then thanked the caller and then closed his phone, more pieces of the jigsaw, look!, go to your rooms and get some rest, I will contact you later with further information as I receive it until that time stay put.

Meena's predicament chapter 25

Meena, woke with a start after crying herself to sleep, raised herself up and swung her legs over the edge of the bed and sat briefly on the side, she then stood up, she noticed that there were clothes nicely laid out at the bottom of the bed, which she examined closely, she decided to take a shower first, then try the clothes on for size, they fitted her, they fitted comfortably, and they felt expensive, she combed her hair and went to the door tried to open it ,but it was locked, she banged a few times, still no reply she tried again; the same, no answer .She returned to the chair beside the bed and sat down. She started to recount the events of the past days, but it was still a little hazy, Jothi, dead, How could that be?. Yes, we ate the same food and drank the same water then why did I not die too. I think something is not quite right, but what!

The door opened and Sita entered and immediately locked the door behind her, how do you feel Meena? A little confused, everything is muddled .1 will tell you the situation as it is ,both you and your friend arrived the other evening at Dr Kumar's clinic suffering from a bad case of food poisoning, the possible result of eating, under cooked sea food at the restaurant you ate at, that same evening, the doctor managed to save you but your friend, Jothi died that same evening .The doctor has instructed me to take you under my wing and to teach you everything about pleasing men, Why?You must understand that it cost a great deal of money to return your friend to Kathmandu and the cost of the doctors services do not come cheaply, and as there is no one else to pay back his investment except you,the doctor has instructed me to teach you how to dress properly with expensive clothes, similar to what you are wearing now,and to train you to entertain his clients when the need be, that way you will be able to repay his kindness towards you.You will remain here and not be let out unless you are accompanied, do I make myself clear! Meena remained silent for a while digesting what she had just heard, can I contact my family? No! was the curt reply, as I said you will remain in this room until I know what to do with you ,so please make your self at home, as this room will be your home for the foreseeable future and at that she turned and left the room, locking the door behind her.

Meena sat quietly for a long time evaluating her situation, she decided to go along with their requests for the time being, and when the opportunity arose, try and escape.

A plan is hatching chapter 26

Early next day DSP Magarabedi, returned to the YMCA, to bring Rupp and his brother Narayan up to speed on the enquiry:

The Cumbala hill clinic is leased to one "Sita Singh Gupta," a high class prostitute and a one time known associate of one Dr. Amit Kumar. "the person that we would like to interview". The lady in Question is known to frequent the Hilton Casino with a male friend of unknown origin, this person we believe to be Dr. Kumar, but we need proof positive proof before we can act, What we need is someone to befriend the couple in order for us to act accordingly, saying that, it is not going to be easy, these people can smell a policeman a mile away, one more thing according to reports Rupp, we believe that your sister may be being held against her wishes in the clinic, for what purpose we do not know,

We need to gain entrance to the clinic to establish credibility to our findings ,however we do not want to alert the Doctor, if indeed it is him ."We are trained for such an eventuality "said Rupp. That may be, but at this juncture we have to tread softly. "That is our situation."

Captain Keith! Exclaimed Rupp!, Captain Keith ,he would help us!, I know he would, and he is a Britisher, what better cover could you get! And I bet he would jump at the opportunity, call him Rupp! Call him, "what can we lose," he can only refuse.

Rupp made the call; he found the Kathmandu telephone contact number of the recruitment centre in his orders which were in his back pack ,After a number of false starts he finally managed to make contact with the captain, "good morning sir", said Rupp, "what can I do for you Corporal"?, "I need your help sir", replied

Rupp, I am currently in Mumbai looking for my sister who we believe is being held against her will, we are working with the local police, however we are in a situation in so much that we need to establish the identity of a certain individual before the police can act ,and the first person we thought of, who could carry out such a request, sir, was you! .OK Corporal , you were there for me when I needed help, "Give me the details". Rupp reiterated all that he knew to date, 1 will arrange to fly to Mumbai on the next available flight ,I will book in to the Mumbai Hilton ,and on my arrival I will make contact with you when I have settled into my room. Rupp, acknowledged the details, thanked the captain then hung up ,Narayan suggested that they should pay a casual visit to the clinic to make ourselves familiar with the area. Detective Magarabedi thought that it was a good idea and that he would drop us close to the area, we would walk the rest of the way so as not to arouse any suspicion,a"good idea" let's go.DSP Magarabedi dropped them a short way off from the clinic and advised them not to bring any attention to them selves, wished them luck, and drove off.

They strolled past the clinic entrance surveyed the premises,stopped briefly to light up a cigarette,to gain that few extra seconds on the subject and walked on into the park near by in a casual manner taking care to make a mental note of the layout of the premises the gateway entrance the guard in his box.etc

Captain Keith arrived at Mumbai international, took a taxi directly to the Hilton where he booked in ,settled himself unpacked his belongings and made the call to the YMCA ,"The presidential suite please" Rupp answered the call ,I have arrived and I am in room 1146 do you want me to come to you or will you come here to me. Silence for a moment."We will come to you sir", and at that he hung up, Narayan called his brother and asked if he could pick them up and take them to the Hilton, can do, I will see you in thirty minutes.

I am with the chief of police, whom I have kept informed of our actions to date. "It would be a feather in his cap ",if the suspect is who we think he is .The chief of police is willing to assist us with man power if required but only with concrete proof.

The captain welcomed us into his room asked us to sit, now ,"what is it you require of me"enquired the captain? This is detective sergeant Magarabedi, said Narayan, "I assume you are brothers ",yes sir, he replied

Narayan,"pleased to meet you, sergeant" Now let's get down to business, said the policeman.

We would like you to befriend a woman, one "Sita Singh Gupta", and her friend, "we need to establish her companions identity, and we need to do it quickly," said Sgt. Magarabedi, not a problem! replied Capt. Keith, but where do I meet These people, Here sir! right here ,they are regular visitors to the casino and they "love to gamble", We can point the pair out to you, after that It would be your job to work your way into their confidence and establish her companions name,

A plan is hatching chapter 26

We would appreciate it, if you could get his finger prints, and a DNA sample to check against our files, which we received from London..They are also suspected of being involved in prostitution ring at the highest level .That is all the information we can give you. "Its enough", said Keith, I will make up a cover story and casually work my charms, "When do I start"?, to-night sir "hopefully! they turn up". Rupp said that he was worried about the whereabouts of his sister. "I can understand your concern Corporal" and I will do my utmost to bring this situation to a quick conclusion, and hopefully find your sister. Business completed they all left.

The captain had just finished showering when the phone rang, Magarabedi here! Sir, captain Keith, The lady and her companion have left the clinic on their way to the Hilton, hopefully, We will follow at a discrete distance and keep you informed as to their destination, good, replied the captain, looks like "game on", The captain continued dressing himself when the phone rang again ."Its me again captain", they are entering the Hilton underground parking, that gives me the opportunity to meet you in the hotel and to single out the couple in question, after that, you are on your own sir, ten minutes later Keith arrived at the reception area all dressed up and raring to go, sergeant Magarabedi was already there a quick hand shake and a few words of caution from the policeman to the captain as they made there way towards the casino ,DS Magarabedi, gestured with a nod of his head towards the couple in question, that's them ,the beauty in the sari and her companion in the evening suit. Sergeant "leave it to me", "I will do my best" and at that he slowly ambled his way alone towards the roulette wheels and his quarry. He felt like James Bond on a secret mission and the thought of helping to apprehend wanted criminals made the excitement all the more intense, I hope I can pull this off ,he thought to himself but before he knew it he was standing next to his quarry.

At the casino chapter 27

The couple were playing roulette at one of the tables, Keith placed himself beside Sita, who was placing single chips on number 21, she placed seven bets on the number before she struck lucky ,"well done miss"!, said Capt. Keith, it must be your lucky number or your age ,she looked at him curiously ,Your English ,no British. Is there a difference ,yes my dear, there is ."I'm a Scot" ,from the highlands of Scotland the British isles are made up of Welsh, Irish ,English ,Scottish and Channel Islanders,we are of differing backgrounds and cultures but we are all British. Very interesting! Said Sita .Keith,! Captain Keith, recent of the Argyle and Sutherland Highlanders, and you are? My name is Sita Singh Gupta, "currently in Mumbai gambling". They both laughed aloud at which point it brought Dr. Kumar to enquire as to the joke, Sita explained quickly and introduced her companion as Amit. They shook hands you are English, nearly, said Keith," I worked in London for a while Captain Keith", said Amit ,Please, call me Richard, its less formal , Richard it is, What brings you to Mumbai Richard? just passing through, they placed a few more bets ,Dr. Kumar asked if Richard would like a drink ,"Yes I would love a scotch" but unfortunately a soft drink will suffice, Why? Enquired Amit, the result of a misspent youth Amit, I love drinking, gambling and beautiful woman, but not necessary in that order, another of my passions is hashing ,an old military tradition which started back in Kuala Lumpur going back before the war, Amit was curious ,"go on Richard I'm intrigued", Richard explained the origins of the hash and went on to tell him that he had just spent the last few days in Goa ,at the "International hash gathering "which happens every four years some where in the world, "a little like the Olympics", Yes I never thought of it like that replied Richard. "Do you smoke hash there Richard"? asked Amit, No, not as a rule, the hashers say that "they are a running club with a drinking problem" ,I see, I see ,said Amit a little unsure, you love drinking and the sport of running, that's about it, a lot of drinking Amit ,But, Alas I, have to be careful, my doctor in England has informed me that my kidneys are shot and that drinking alcohol is forbidden along with a few other vices, so a soft drink is my limit,! Dr. Kumar paused for a moment then looked at Richard, What if I could help you there?, what do you mean? I mean, that, I know someone who could help you, but at a price! That's kind of you Amit but I don't quite follow, said Richard pretending to be a little surprised at the doctors offer, "a new kidney Richard", so that you could resume your drinking, but at reduced quantities. Let me think about that Amit, what would it cost?, a rough price Oh!say $20,000 US. Richard went quiet for a while, that's not a bad price to pay for a new kidney, but can you guarantee success!" Every time Richard" every time. They carried on the conversation about kidneys until Richard turned the conversation gently to cricket and other general topics so as not to be over keen on Kidney transplants in case the doctor smelled a rat. Sita was quite happy to lose money at the tables, this allowed Richard to build a rapport with the good doctor and gain his confidence, Amit drank whiskey steadily and the captain kept his eye on the empty glasses for further recovery for DNA testing and finger prints. Sita started to get bored losing and eventually came over and said that she had a task back at the clinic which needed her attention and would like to go home as it was getting late, as she felt tired, very good my dear! said Kumar, and at that both men stood up and shook hands, Dr Kumar, handing a card to

Richard with his contact details before leaving, think over my proposal Richard, and call me, The couple left, Richard immediately took out a handkerchief from his pocket and wrapped it around a whiskey glass that Amit had been drinking from and put it gently in his jacket pocket. When he was sure that they had gone he made his way through the casino into the hotels main foyer into the lift and up his room. As he entered his room the phone rang, Magarabedi here!, "I see that they have left the casino sir", did you have any success ,yes! sergeant replied Richard I have a whiskey glass for you, can you send someone to collect it so that your forensic people can examine it for finger prints, right away sir, said Magarabedi.

End Game chapter 28

Captain Keith was preparing to go for breakfast, when a knock came on the door, opened it, and was greeted by a policeman, good morning sir, the police Commissioner has asked me to take you to the Police headquarters at Lokmanya Marg.

I was just on my way to get breakfast, It is urgent sir, I have others waiting out in the car, captain Keith pulled on his jacket and followed the young policeman out of the hotel to a waiting car, as he slid into the front seat he was greeted with a good morning sir!, Chandra and Magarabedi were dressed in casual clothes, I didn't recognise you both without your uniforms on. Is there any news?, I'm afraid I am as much in the dark as you sir, but I am thinking that all will be revealed at police headquarters, the rest of the journey was quiet each trying to work out what was up,

when they arrived at the compound they were ushered up the stairs to a large planning room where detective Magarabedi, and a few other police officers were deep in conversation around a large round table, at the appearance of the group they all stood up and introductions were made by DSP Magarabedi.

The chief of police motioned to the group to sit and make themselves comfortable. "If you are all seated I shall begin".

On my instructions Captain Keith was asked to help us with our inquiries into the identity of a very dangerous man, one Dr Amit Kumar, a surgeon of repute engaged in the illegal practice of kidney transplants for large sums of money, we can now confirm that the finger prints extracted from a whiskey glass obtained from the bar at the Hilton casino, last night, were indeed belonging to the person much sought after by all the police forces throughout the Indian sub continent.

We at the request of the Nepalese police, Detective sergeant Magarabedi has been working in close cooperation with our force and as such we have established the exact whereabouts of the suspect and his entourage. They are operating from an address in Cumbala hills, currently the Cumbala Hill clinic located at Pantai road near to Johnson and Johnson gardens. We have appropriated a copy of the layout of the premises, which I have here for us to study and to prepare our method of entry in order to catch this Dr Amit Kumar and his associates, normally we would not involve the public in what is strictly a police matter but Corporal Chandra ,can identify ,some one," his sister", who we believe is being held against her will, and Captain Keith who has given us this opportunity to apprehend this criminal, also, these gentlemen are skilled at effectively gaining entry into heavily protected premises the like we are facing. Gentlemen!

Captain Richard Keith .The captain walked around the table and started to study the plans five ten minutes passed then he said I think I can effect a plan which can make the entry as straight forward as can be. Simply put, I have a contact telephone number for the infamous doctor I will call him and ask to have a meeting with him at his premises on the pretext of him arranging a possible operation.

As you can see from the schematics there is only one way in, storming the premises would alert the occupants inside and if they have a an escape plan, for such an eventually, they just might disappear before we gain access to the inner buildings and all your work would be in vain .1 suggest that if I can arrange an appointment as proposed my men and your men, be quietly positioned inside the park opposite the entrance where you can get a clear view of the gate, when I arrive and the gates are opened we will arrange for the vehicle to stall half way through the gates signaling your opportunity to rush through with the minimum of noise, there are number of sets of buildings ,so by designating who goes where the operation can be carried out with the maximum effectiveness with the minimum of fuss .That's' the theory gentlemen ,we do not know what is in there I would advise the use of stun grenades for causing loud noises which tend to confuse those that are not expecting unwelcome visitors

End game chapter 28

The chief of police acknowledged Capt. Keith's appraisal of the situation and said that it all hangs on your telephone call being successful, there is only one way to find out said Capt. Keith, I will make the call. Sergeant Magarabedi handed him his mobile phone, use this captain ,are we in agreement, if the doctor allows me to visit his premises this evening ,we go, yes captain ,that is affirmative, said the chief

Captain Keith called the number it rang for a few moments then a voice said yes ,who is calling it's Richard Keith ,Amit, we talked last night .1 remember said the doctor what can I do for you Richard? he said guardedly ,about what you said about the friend who could possibly help me ,Amit I am flying out in the morning and I would like to understand more before I go ,the money is no object just the usual questions that's all.

Can you come around seven thirty this evening my address is on the card, the taxi driver should find the place with little difficulty, seven thirty it is Amit ,I look forward to meeting you again ,with that he closed the phone. So, gentlemen you all heard seven thirty to night that's our cue. The police chief spoke next I will select our teams and prepare them with your instructions and the Modus Operandi, (method of operation) I suggest that we meet here in police HQ at five o'clock for further deployment on this matter. The police officer who brought you will take you back to your respective hotels .A policeman posing as a taxi driver will collect Captain Keith at the Hilton at 1630 hours and take him to the clinic my men along with our guests will be taken quietly to the park in small groups so as not to cause alarm then await the taxi, carrying Capt. Keith, good luck! And may god be on our side!

The taxi arrived at the gate, on schedule the driver pumped the horn, the gates slowly opened once they were fully opened the taxi, slowly started to enter the engine stalled, the driver made futile efforts to restart ,the guard left the security of his security box and slowly made his way over to the stationary vehicle. just as the police and the soldiers swarmed through the gates.

The attackers rushed towards there designated targets hurtling stun grenades through the windows and doors to cause as much distraction as possible , The occupants were taken off guard as the police teams came pouring in and rounding them up, and yelling for them to get down on the floor with their hands behind their backs. Captain Keith leapt out of the vehicle knocking the guard to the floor, upholstered his army revolver and proceeded to the living quarters as fast as he could with Sergeant Chandra hot on his heals waving a pick axe handle and striking the guard over the head as he passed, rendering him unconscious

Captain Keith entered the room; he immediately caught sight of a wall panel half opened, which he quickly passed through ,he immediately came across Dr. Kumar stuffing money into a large back pack .You bastard Keith !, he yelled ,You fooled me into thinking that you genuinely needed help ,and all the time planning my demise , Let me go ,Please!, and I will give you money, Lots of money ,said Doctor Kumar. "You are under arrest Kumar,"! at which Kumar swung the backpack at the captain who made an evasive move to avoid the strike, Rupp at the same time made a fierce jab to the doctors stomach with his pick axe handle which brought the good doctor to his knees, Where is my sister yelled Rupp?, Where is my sister;? Dr Kumar who was on his knees pointed to a door at the end of the passage, before collapsing in a pile at the feet of the captain," Rupp proceeded towards the door"cautiously with pick handle at the ready.

Meena had been sitting on the edge of the bed, contemplating what to do when the building began to tremble, a series of loud bangs followed, she became frightened, so she hid under the bed for what seemed an eternity, the door flew open and she could see a pair of army boots in front of her eyes. Silence, which seemed to last for an eternity then a voice said is there anyone here!, if there is ,come out at once!, the voice sounded very much like her brother Rupp ,but, he was in England a surge of emotion gripped her ,and she began to cry.

Meena! is that you, Its me Rupp! your brother, I have been searching all over this city for you!, for god's sake, "I hope you're here"!,Rupp!, came the reply I'm here!, I'm here ,under the bed, she crawled out from under the bed and jumped at him ,crying I can't believe its you, its really you, They want me to entertain men to pay back the expenses for sending my friend Jothi, who died ,back to Nepal, no! its not true, its not true. Jothi, your friend is in the Nair hospital recovering from the loss of a kidney, "she is safe," and so are you sister, Rupp stepped back to have a close look at his sister , my you have changed sister you look absolutely stunning in that dress ,honestly you look like you just came out of a Bollywood film, he then gave her another hug to reassure her that she was not dreaming

When Rupp and Meena emerged from the building into the yard, the police were loading their prisoners into the back of the Black Maria's to be taken to police HQ for further questioning ,

The television media who, for some reason had been tipped off about the impending police raid at the clinic were waiting outside on the opposite side of the street to interview anyone who emerged from the premises ,the bright lights and the flashing bulbs were a little disconcerting to Rupp and Meena as they ventured out through the gates, Rupp squeezed Meenas hand ,look sister, just pretend you are a film star and this is your opportunity to shine ,Remember Meena that the whole world will be watching this on the news and if you want to catch the eye of an influential Bollywood mogul now is your opportunity sister, act like you have never acted before, show the world what Meena Chandra is made of.

Meena grasped the opportunity with both hands; she smiled at the cameras and was ever ready to answer any and all questions put to her by the television interviewers with the utmost tact and diplomacy.

A few days later Jothi was informed that Binod Chaudry, had told the police everything ,and that because he had only paid 50% of the fees the remainder , the balance of 1.5 m ruppees he was going to give to Jothi, he stated ,"I cannot give back the life saving organ",! that she unwittingly parted with, but I can make her life a little easier in the future with this money.

A few days later as they waited in the lounge at Mumbai international ,for their flight back to Kathmandu, the "Mumbai posts", heading read :**"ring leader of international kidney racketeering gang apprehended"** Rajan Parayan, "had been apprehended at Kathmandu airport on his return from Mumbai on the advice of Mumbai police.

Franklin Pate chapter 29

Franklin Pate, was putting the final touches to his latest block buster movie when his eye caught the local news, in particular an article on a police raid on a clinic, on the outskirts of the city ,the interviewer was interviewing a stunningly beautiful girl who immediately caught his imagination, her natural affinity with the camera and the strength of character which she showed considering the ordeal that she had just gone through Nur ! he cried to his personal secretary, That girl ,"The one in the news"! get her? She is ideal for the role of Nan in the new Movie "Nan & Kana,"his latest masterpiece, yes sir! she retorted immediately!

Nur rang the local television station for the information as to the whereabouts of the interviewer and the girl in question ,to our knowledge, she was returning to Nepal on the evening flight, from Mumbai International, if you hurry you may be able to get hold of her, before she leaves the country, thank you, and at that Nur rang off.

She immediately rang the information desk at Mumbai International, and requested that they Page a miss Meena Chandra, as it was of the utmost importance ,"who should I say is calling", I am Nur Hadayati personal secretary to Franklin Pate the Mumbai based movie maker, replied Nur, there was silence for a few moments then in an excited voice, I have seen all his movies they are wonderful, Please, please make the announcement miss err. "Ranti! is my name"! Ranti said Nur , it is of the utmost importance,-- just a moment Nur she replied." Calling miss Meena Chandra", calling miss Meena Chandra" ,there is an urgent call for you at the reception, please contact the reception desk immediately "Thank you"!

Meena was surprised at the mention of her name on the loud speaker system , she turned to Rupp, and said, Rupp who would be looking for me at the airport ,"I do not know" sister, but I would suggest that you go to the reception and find out before we board the plane to fly home. Meena made her way to the reception desk wondering who would be calling her; at the reception she informed the girl that she was Meena Chandra, oh! miss Chandra there is a call from Mr. Franklin Pates secretary and she wants to speak to you personally, she said excitedly, Thank you miss, and at that Meena was handed the phone ,hello who's calling said Meena, My name is Nur Hadayati, I am the personal secretary to Mr. Franklin Pate, the well known movie Mogul ,he has instructed me to contact you personally and to ask you to come directly to his home, I will arrange for a limousine to collect you and your party from the airport and convey you to Mr. Pates studio's which are situated in the grounds of his home. Miss Nur, "we are about to leave on the next flight to Nepal", do not worry about that Meena ,I will arrange for Mr. Pates private aircraft to convey you and your party back to Nepal when you have concluded your business with him. Make your way to the entrance of the departure hall and look for a large white stretch limousine license number "Mogul 1",the driver has been instructed to expect you and your party ,he will convey you to your destination, and I will meet you when you arrive, I look forward to meeting you Meena and at that Nur replaced the handset on the cradle and informed her boss that she had successfully carried out his request.

As Meena and her party emerged from the terminal building they saw the white limousine pulled up outside the VIP parking area, Rupp approached the driver and enquired if he was from Franklin Pates studios the answer was affirmative, and at that Rupp, beckoned to his sister and his friend to approach and enter the vehicle. The interior was white leather with plenty of leg room for them to stretch out, a fridge with cold drinks, blinds to shut the outside world out a telephone which suddenly sprang into life Meena picked up the phone and sheepishly said "hello" !,Franklin Pate, speaking ,is that Meena he enquired ,Yes it is replied Meena ,I suppose you are wondering why I requested your presence at my studios Meena, Well it is all good news but I will wait until you arrive before I explain my proposal have a comfortable journey and I will see you presently, and with that he closed the phone. Meena explained to Rupp what was said, and the rest of the journey was in silence.

The limousine turned right into tree lined avenue and continued towards the huge white colonial house situated at at the end of this magnificent drive ,the limo stopped under a pillared canopy and the driver got out and walked to the rear and opened the door,Rupp then Magga exited first then beckoned Meena to come out ,as she did Nur appeared at the doorway and moved towards Meena ,"I can see why my boss is keen to meet you, you are a real beauty ",sorry ,I am Nur,I am Mr Pates private secretary and I am at your disposal I will be your your guide and I will be at your service ,anything you require just ask and I will be only to pleased to comply with your wishes, I can understand your concerns Meena ,but Mr. Pate will explain his intentions and make everything clear this way please just follow me. Nur, led them through corridors full of pictures of famous Bollywood stars, their famous movies, with silver and gold awards and all hung in row after row ,it was mind boggling for someone to see such an astonishing array of accolades and the movie hierarchy of Bollywood greats it was exciting and nerve racking at the same time her head was spinning

."Here we are"!, said Nur as she ushered them into a small sitting area ,Please ,be seated Mr. Pate will be with you shortly ,I will arrange for some refreshments and with that she left them Almost immediately Franklin appeared introduced himself to Meena, Rupp and Maga, Motioned them to be seated ,He expressed his delight in Meena,s coming so promptly, and complimented her in her beautify he explained that he had just completed his latest musical and felt sure that Meena would be suited the part of the heroine, with careful handling and promotion she could become a mega star. I have prepared an outline proposal for your perusal and if you agree I will have my lawyers draw up a contract for your signature.

The basic outline is thus Mumbai studios will pay you an amount of two million rupee's per year, cover all costs and make you an allowance for clothing for a period of two years after which time a new contract will be drawn up when you or your manager will make a new proposal which will be of mutual benefit to all concerned   The door opened and a turbaned young male servant entered with a tray of tea and soft drinks ,Meena expressed her gratitude to Franklin who acknowledged her gesture but explained that she would have to work very hard as making films was a very arduous and competitive profession ,Rupp explained that Meena loved singing and dancing and that at any opportunity such as that Franklin was offering was her most cherished desire and believed that Meena would be a credit to his studios, "I agree with you Rupp", replied Franklin,

I have spoken with Nur and she will arrange for you all to be flown back to Nepal in my private plane, whenever you are ready to leave ,and as we are in agreement I will arrange for my lawyers to draw up the papers for your signature Meena! will you leave all your contact details with Nur as she will be in continuous contact with you as she is your link to the studios and myself "Do you have any requests ", yes just one can your driver take us to the hospital before we fly back, of course Meena you want to see your friend to tell her the good news.

The limousine pulled up outside the hospital, the driver alighted, and came to the rear and again opened the door, Meena stepped out and was immediately greeted like royalty by the hospital staff, which frightened her a little, she realised that her life would change quite drastically from now on, "for better or worse", she did not know, She was directed to where Jothi was ,she was surprised to see Jothi up and walking around ,when they saw each other they embraced like they had not seen each other for long time both girls at the same time blurted out," I have news for you",Jothi spoke first ,she said Binaud Chaudry had come to the hospital to visit her about an hour ago and said that he would be paying her a lump sum for her kidney ,He said he could not return the organ which had saved his life and that he would be eternally grateful to her, and to prove his gratitude he would be drawing up a cheque in her name to the value of two million Nepalese rupees a small fortune, the cheque would be paid to her the moment she returned to Kathmandu. Meena told Jothi all about her meeting with Franklin Pate and his proposal, both girls again embraced each other and cried tears of joy, both said that: god is watching over us,.They chatted for a while until the driver appeared and informed Meena that the pilot had requested their presence at the airport as soon possible , with that the girls kissed and hugged, before they parted with promises of seeing each other soon.

After passport control Meena, Rupp and Maga were met by the pilot, who introduced himself he then proceeded to accompany them to the private parking area where they boarded the Leer jet .They were shown to their seats by the stewardess and advised to strap themselves in prior to take off.

Back to Nepal chapter 30

The Leer jet touched down at Kathmandu International and taxied to the VIP parking area ,The pilot advised his passengers that they had arrived at their destination and that they should remain seated until the immigration staff had checked their passports and given them the all clear to proceed to the terminal VIP lounge before transshipment to their home ,the pilot also informed them that taxis had been ordered to covey them to their destinations.

Rupp embraced Maga and said he would see him at the recruiting centre in a few days after he returned home to see his family and again thanked him for all his and his brothers help in saving his sister ,then he entered the taxi, Meena kissed Maga on the cheek and again thanked him for all his help then she entered the taxi with her brother for the journey to their parents home and a good nights sleep. It was the first time they had been alone together since the rescue and everything that had transpired since then, she put her head on Rupps shoulder and fell fast asleep safe in the presence of her brother "her hero". she was having a lovely dream about Bollywood and a romance with a mega star, when

Meena woke with a startle, the taxi hit a few potholes on the road leading up to their home, she quickly realised where she was, and that she had dozed off for a moment, she busily tided herself before being re-united with her parents, They both were expecting to return to a quiet house ,but as they left the taxi they sensed that something was amiss, Rupp gently pushed the front door, it open hesitantly and made an eerie creek! Rupp went into a defensive mode when a mighty cry of "welcome home Rupp our hero"! and "Meena our beautiful Daughter soon to be a Bollywood star", they were both taken back a little with the reception ,but never the less happy to be greeted by all their relatives and friends and half the village .

The party went on well into the early morning ,both Rupp and Meena being continually quizzed ,Rupp about the British army, especially from young Silvio, and Meena about her meeting with a Bollywood legend over and over again until they both fell fast asleep on the floor next to each other.

Over the next few days Rupp and Meena spent as much time in each others company they both talked about their futures and their hopes and dreams , and both agreeing that their futures seemed to be taking shape ,A far cry from last year when Rupp was hoping that he would pass the initiation tests for the British , and Meena worried that her future lay in the carpet industry or worse, but her dreams and aspirations were in a whole different world ,a world that she could only dream about, now to become a reality

Rupps leave was at an end he kissed his mother and shook his fathers hand as he embraced him ,Meena said that she would accompany him to the recruiting station in Kathmandu ,As they entered the taxi Meenas phone rang it was Nur, calling to notify her that the contract had been drawn up for her perusal and signature and that she had arranged dancing and singing lessons plus publicity photo shoots, etc for the film ,and the best bit was that "Ganesh"the most sought after actor in Bollywood was to be her co-star ."That is wonderful news!," when do you want me to return to Mumbai?",replied Meena, I have arranged for a taxi to pick you up at ten O'clock to-morrow morning to take you to the airport, and from there be flown to Mumbai international by Franklin's private jet, "I look forward to seeing you again", said Nur ,until tomorrow Meena,

Then she rang off.

The taxi pulled up outside the recruiting centre, Meena and Rupp stepped out,Meena embraced her brother and said her farewells just as Captain Keith appeared ,"Meena I have something for you"!he said ,it is a miniature replica of Sir William Wallace's sword, he was a famous Scottish hero, the sword will protect you at all times ,She accepted the gift gracefully put her hands together and bowed gracefully and immediately put it around her neck smiled thanked him again, then she entered the taxi and headed back home, she experienced that same bite of loneliness when Rupp went off to England to complete his army training however ,the excitement of starting in the film industry still played a major part in her thoughts ,she wondered ,what type of clothes to purchase," I will ask Nur for her advice and guidance on this matter", she thought, the taxi arrived at the house ,she paid for the journey and went for a walk down the lane ,the same lane she used to dream about ,and now her dream was taking shape.

To-morrow she would begin to live her dream," what an exciting prospect."

Recruiting the new intake chapter 31

At the meeting of the selection of marshals for the Dholo race, capt. Keith, designated Sgt. Rupp Chandra a position at the top of a long incline which had the advantage of an overall view of the approaching runners for a mile before they started the long upward climb ,a real obstacle for unfit runners the kind of obstacle which would separate the men from the boys.

Rupp made his way to his allotted position, as he climbed it brought back flashes of when he met the obstacle the year before and remembered that although the climb was long and steep ,he was not daunted, as he had ran up it many times during his own training sessions ,he reached his designated position and turned around ,immediately being confronted by the view of the lofty peaks covered in a swirl of white clouds which hid the tops giving the mountains a stunted look ,which was misleading in a way as these were the highest mountains in the world. views to be admired, the changing weather made every moment a pleasure as the vistas were changing minute by minute revealing falling waterfalls and beautifully wooded slops of natural beautify, something Rupp had not realised he had missed since joining the army, they brought an instant tug at his heart the United Kingdom and Afghanistan , had their own natural sights but in his mind they did not compare with the mountains of home.

Rupp took up his position and waited for the first runners to arrive,to pass the time he thought about Meena and wondered how she was coping with her new opportunity in the film industry ,and hopefully her bad experience in Mumbai was behind her and that her confidence in her own ability to do well in her new career had not been dented. I will try to keep in contact with her as much as possible thought Rupp, but then again I know that my sister, she would not let a day pass without contacting me or our parents , a thoughtful and considerate woman I have never met ,then I only have experience of two woman ,my mother and my sister

A sudden clap of thunder followed a few seconds later by a click and bolt of lightening , brought Rupp back to reality ,the rain came pouring down like a river ,Rupp pulled out his army poncho pulled it over his head repositioned his hat and sat down inside his small lean to, facing the slope ,although he was fairly dry in his shelter ,he thought of the runners who had to continue with their test now made even harder ,at that moment the first runners started to appear at the foot of the hill , although the rain was falling heavily the surface was wet but still solid a short way down with enough grip for the early runners, the tail enders on the other hand might have difficulty climbing especially when the ground gets rutted up giving little or no grip .Rupp noted that the majority of participants had succeeded in reaching the top ,but ,according to his schedule one more runner was still to come ,after a considerable time had passed Rupp thought that he had either given up or had not started the race ,the rain became more violent making the ground disappear as it bounced back into the air creating a haze due to its great force, "I will make my way back to the starting post when the rain subsides thought Rupp "suddenly through the haze came a lone runner plodding on slowly but with an air of determination ,he started the long climb slipping and sliding one way then the other in the rutted and slippery surface which was well churned up by both runners and the torrential rain ,on up he trudged a small lonely figure all alone in his quest for success ,Rupp admired at his persistence and as the runner almost reached the top ,he lost his footing ,made a futile attempt at grasping at exposed roots, but to no avail ,he missed and started to roll over and over again all the way back to the bottom of the slope ,when he reached the bottom he struggled to his feet shook himself pulled his back pack onto his shoulders and looked up and again started the long trudge back up the slope ,Rupps heart went out to him he knew how he would have felt at that moment ,all his training to succeed to join the British army fast disappearing in front of him , such an obstacle would make or break you at that moment ,the runner again trudged up up towards his goal , up up he fought slipping and sliding and getting weaker and weaker in the process but determined to reach the top half way up he lost his footing yet again and he slithered all the way down to the bottom ,Rupp realised that he was not going to manage the slope and his bid was rapidly coming to a close ,the runner made one more feeble attempt at the edifice but could only manage a few yards before he slipped again only this time he just lay there completely exhausted

Rupp made his way down to the dishevelled runner who now was on his back facing the sky and breathing heavily, as Rupp neared he thought he recognised the figure and as he neared he became more convinced that it was one of the boys from his village ,he was shocked to see Samri a fourteen year old a boy who lived close to Rupps parents house ",what are you doing here Samri "exclaimed Rupp, you are too young to join the army! ,but the boy did not hear his words as he was crying at his frustration at not completing the trail, Rupp pulled him to his feet , removed his pack put his arm around the distraught lad and explained that even if he had completed the race he would not have been accepted into the army as a recruit as he was underage ,you need to be eighteen, you are only fourteen ,Rupp went on to say to Samri that he should be proud of himself as it took sheer determination to achieve what he had accomplished at such a tender age and that if he keeps on training when he gets to the required age of eighteen, he should pass the initiation tests with ease and that he Sgt Rupp Chandra ,would be looking out for him .The boy stopped crying and thanked Rupp for all his consideration ,you know Samri ,Its men like you that the British army needs you are a credit to the Nepalese nation

Back at the recruiting office captain Keith ,had an announcement to make ,gentlemen I have received orders from the M.O.D. that our next posting is to Iraq, I have chosen my officers and non - commissioned officers who will accompany me on our next escapade into harms way , all relevant information will be posted on the notice boards for your information,

Meena's progress chapter 32

Meena was so happy! her progress in her new career was progressing well, she would periodically pinch herself to make sure that it was real and not a dream .Her dancing and singing lessons had been of special significance ,she felt good that her voice had improved beyond her imagination and her dancing much more graceful, according to her tutors , her outings with Nur had shown her a whole new outlook to purchasing clothes, before she could only afford saris at the cheaper end of the of the market ,now, money was no object to her purchases, she felt a little embarrassed in the beginning at the expensive clothes which Nur had advised her to buy, Nur put her mind at ease by explaining that she had to dress for her public and that in the future she would be an obstacle of admiration and that she would have to dress accordingly ,the press would be critical of everything she wore and everything she would say and do ,

Paul Pettergen, the American entrepreneur ,who was Franklin's major investor in the new film was curios about Franklin's new protégé ,he had read the script and was enthusiastic about his new venture He listened intently as Franklin's enthused about Meena, and asked to see any promotional material on her ,she recently did some promotional shots for the film ,whereupon Franklin produced some of the first stills of Meena posing in various positions ,"Paul was aghast", Franklin, you certainly have an eye for beauty," I would like to take her for a meal" said Paul, can you arrange a meeting for me .Franklin was not in favour of Paul entertaining Meena , he knew from past experiences with Paul's attitude of disregard for the feelings and culture of his young starlets ,but Paul was very persuasive and assured Franklin that he would be on his best behaviour. Franklin reneged , he knew he had to keep Paul sweet.

A few days latter Meena returned from location shooting, Nur informed her of her pending date with Paul Pettergen, and advised her to keep him at arms length ,he is the kind of man who likes woman to fall over themselves for him he is arrogant and selfish so be on your guard .

Although Nur was advising Meena ,Meena could not contain herself from telling her all about Ganesh, her leading man, I can understand why woman fall at his feet ,he is so talented and so handsome ,I was expecting him to be full of himself because of his popularity ,on the contrary he was extremely modest and considerate ,for the first time in my life I met a man who was as thoughtful and considerate of others like my brother "Rupp."

To-night Meena ,I have arranged for you to dine with Paul Pettergen ,a major financial contributor in the film and it is Franklin's wish that you entertain him at the Hilton,The reservation is for nine   o,clock Mr Pettergen will meet you in the bar at eight o,clock ,to enjoy a few drinks before sharing a quiet meal together in the restaurant,He may want to go on to a show later but that would be up to you ,good luck and have a good meal.

Meena returned to the Hilton to prepare herself for her encounter with the American, she felt honoured yet scared at the thought of entertaining a business partner of Franklin's should she be herself or should she be business like and unapproachable, she decided to be friendly but not too! Friendly in case he got the wrong impression..

Meena came out of the shower patted herself dry ,sprayed on channel no5 and chose the most expensive sari in the wardrobe, and laid it on the bed brushed dried her beautiful raven black hair with the hotel hair-drier and slipped into her choice of evening ware. She gracefully made her way down to the bar quietly, she gently pushed open the door and glided into the lounge bar ,every head without exception turned to admire this vision, Meena felt her face flush, she was as yet not used to this kind of admiration, as she stood there slightly embarrassed a young waiter enquired as to her name .

Meena Chandra , yes Meena he replied, Mr Pettergen is expecting you miss, follow me please as he escorted her to a private table, Paul was fixated by this vision of beauty as she approached his table, he felt all the eyes in the room looking on enviously at this lucky man about to be entertained by this Indian beautify.

Introductions made ,Paul ordered a bottle of champagne and two glasses,from the young waiter at which point Meena interjected ",I am sorry Mr Pettergen", but I do not drink alcohol, a glass of sparkling water would be nice, as you please Meena ,your wish is my desire .Paul was eager to know all about Meena ,where she came from her family how she came to meet Franklin Pate the questions were endless Meena told him as much as she wanted him to know ,just before they made their way to the restaurant he asked her if she was associated with someone she said that she was too! Busy with the the new film and all that she was doing that she had no time to think about romance ,"So there may be a chance for me, "Meena did not answer as she did not fully understand the implication behind the statement .

Paul continued to comment on her beauty at every occasion during their time in the lounge and at the meal table, Meena felt uncomfortable with the continued barrage of compliments and tried to steer the conversation on to another topic ,tell me about your self Paul ,where in America are you from ,are you married, do you have children ?,Paul went in to rhymes about himself and how he started in business and how he met Franklin on and on but never a mention about his wife and children ,it was like they did not exist ,Paul continued drinking one whiskey after another ,but maintained his composure at all times the meal was served and like the conversation came and went ,sipping on a brandy Paul suggested that they go on to another venue or a show or would Meena prefer to go to the casino, to be honest Mr Pettergen ,sorry Paul I would like to return to my room as I am very tired, I have had anenjoyable evening with you and hope you do not mind I have just returned from filming outstation and have barely rested for a week or so ,Paul was angry, I have gone to all this work and expense into giving you an enjoyable evening and you repay me with running of to your room at the first opportunity, at which point he turned his back on her muttering and waltzed of towards the bar . Meena felt a little guilty but she was tired , she made her way to the elevator, she entered alone ,pressed the button to close the door and the button to her floor ,the elevator seemed to take forever to reach her floor, the door opened and she stepped out slowly and made her way to her room removed her pass card swiped it in the slot and the door opened

Meena was suddenly and violently pushed from behind and catapulted into the room which was in total darkness grabbed by the hair and thrown onto the bed ,"bitch ,you little bitch," play games with me ,Ill show you who is boss came a gruff voice a hand came around her throat and another pulling at her sari trying to rip it from her body Meena tried to scream but to no avail the swiftness of the assault was so sudden and aggressive, coupled with the sheer terror that she felt no words came out of her mouth ,she tried with both hands to pull the intruders hands from around her neck ,she felt her legs were being forced apart all happening so fast, suddenly her hand felt the sword necklace that captain Keith had given to her she pulled the necklace from her neck and proceeded to make stabbing motions at the face of her attacker ,he screamed fell backwards off the bed holding his face which was pouring blood ,realising his victim was fighting back he turned and ran from the room Meena pulled herself off the bed crying and shaking like a leaf she managed to find the light switch turned on the lights and went directly to the phone dialling the reception and screaming out what had happened to her Meena sat on the edge bed sobbing her heart out ,the hotel security soon arrived ,knocked on the door and entered Meena was crying and trying to wipe the imaginary intruder off her body, immediately he called his colleagues to stop anyone leaving the hotel and to inform the police He then informed the reception that he was transferring the young lady in question to the presidential suite and securing the room for the police to check for clues as to who committed such a vicious attack on their guest.

Nur and Franklin soon appeared to comfort Meena and to further understand what had happened Meena. explained that she spent most of the evening with Paul Pettergen they had a cordial evening together and as Paul suggested to continue the evening she quietly refused and returned to her room as she was about to enter the incident happened.

After a lot of discussion, it was decided that Meena remained at the Hilton with a guard outside her door and that Nur would remain with her until the following day.

After a sleepless night Meena informed Nur that she

would like the incident to be kept quiet ,as it would give the hotel a bad name which was a little unfair and that as she was just starting out in the film industry, the publicity would not be good for the studio, Franklin also informed Meena that from now on she would have her own bodyguard .

It occurred to Meena that being attractive to men had its good points but it also had an ugly side especially when your are in the public eye , she realised that life in the future would not be plain sailing as she had dreamed about.

Welcome to Iraq chapter 33

Rupp stepped out the rear end of the argosy into the afternoon sun to capture his first glimpse of Basra ,as he scanned the horizon he was expecting to see sand dunes, and camels but it was totally flat and sandy as far as the eye could see unlike Nepal not a hill in sight, he picked up his gear and made his way to the waiting buses ,which would transport them to Base 1, their new home for the next three months, on the way Rupp noted that the local inhabitants were waving to the soldiers on the bus ,a sure sign that the locals were in favour of the foreign troops on there streets ,hopefully, thought Rupp that would make our job all the more easier ,but people are unpredictable as well he knew and reassured himself to be on guard at all times .as rogue mullahs can incite the locals with a few chosen words, and change the mood very quickly.

Base1 base was a jumble of old buildings cobbled together with safety hoardings(concrete blocks)with razor wire atop to form an inner perimeter and an outer defensive ring which was heavily fortified with staggered walls to protect the base against attack from vehicles filled with munitions from ramming into the protected living area with the intention of exploding and killing as many of our troops as possible .We were designated our billeting area as soon as we arrived , told to make ourselves as comfortable as best we can as "Al Qaeda , regularly fire home made missiles at the base, "just to keep us on our toes ",quipped a squaddie

Assembly called , we mustered inside an old building which had been the recipient of many a welcoming rocket ,Captain Keith informed us of our duties ,we would patrol the streets in the evenings and train the local conscripts during the day ,something that we were experienced at from our Afghanistan tour ,

Suddenly sirens went off ,soldiers were running for cover, Captain Keith coolly and calmly advised us to remain in our seats and ignore the melee that was happening outside ,The insurgents so far as I have been advised are poor shots and as such their aim and trajectories normally meant that the missiles landed short or overshoot the base ,occasionally, but very occasionally, they were successful ,but rarely, Rupp like the rest of the company trusted their leader ,"anyhow" thought Rupp, where would we run we had just arrived and had no time to locate the shelters .The sirens soon fell quiet , and the all clear sounded. Corporal Magarabedi, advised that it was "kind of the terrorists to welcome us to Basra "with a show of fireworks everyone laughed ,and the tension was released.

We soon settled into our routine of evening forays through the city, we would walk in two lines on opposite sides of the street spaced 3 to 4 meters apart ,we interacted with the locals as much as possible as a softly softly approach was the order of the day ,the local inhabitants were reasonably friendly but they viewed our regiment as something of an enigma as we were much shorter than the paras or the guards, however we understood their ways more clearly as many of our troops were Muslim, the evening routines normally passed off with little disturbance ,however on a couple occasions we were fired at ,but the perpetrators were soon gone .On these patrols I often wondered how my sister was in her new profession, I received a letter telling me that the film was going well and that her co star Ganesh was the perfect partner and she understood why the women all loved him," much like you brother" ,he is modest and humble but very versatile. "A man of action "

The prime minister is paying us a visit was the latest

rumour circulating around the base ,this made us feel very important the chief of the armed forces coming to Iraq to visit the front line troops ,"what a moral booster" a few days later a chopper came down in the middle of the compound as I was crossing, out popped the prime minister, he walked over to me and shook my hand for a moment, I did not know what to do except stand back and salute ,he smiled and said :"carry on sergeant", he then ushered inside the main building by his bodyguards, I was astounded ,the prime minister ,Tony Blair, shook my hand ,"this is something to tell my grand children".

The visit by the prime minister gave the garrison such a lift, plus he left with promises of more sophisticated equipment,(night vision goggles)etc. for days after we were walking on clouds ,the situation in the city seemed to be peaceful ,we were aroused from our lethargy with an attack on a police station, the insurgents rammed the building with a truck full of explosives killing all inside The news was devastating ,as we were wrongly thinking that we were winning the battle for hearts and minds ,the people needed something to hang on to but the insurgents were making sure that the peace would not last .

The day started as usual ,but after the incident of the day before the recruits stayed away ,Captain Keith advised that there would be no training schedule today ,instead we would patrol the streets in the afternoon as we needed to show a presence, to give the populace a sense of security ,"god knows they needed something", as they lacked even the basic amenities, we felt for them, the patrol moved out as usual in two columns, spaced well apart, the majority of locals were friendly but today there were few people abroad and the tension you could cut with a knife ,instead of the usual friendly greetings people would vanish behind closed doors as soon as they saw us approaching ,Corporal Magarabedi ,my close friend said Rupp," I don't know about you but I feel that something frightening is about happen ,"I was about to reassure him that we were all on edge due to the incident yesterday, when a mortar landed in the middle of the road ,we all dived for cover ,as the mortars came raining down killing a number of the local inhabitants instantly ,two children were standing in the middle of the road screaming for all they were worth ,I immediately surveyed up and down the street no gunmen ,and without thinking I ran across the road at the same time scooping up the two little girls in my arms as I passed ,I ran straight at an open alley and deposited the children on the ground before using my rifle butt to break open a window put the children in and put my finger to my lips indicating for them to be quiet ,the mortars came again followed by a Toyota pick up with hooded bandits shooting wildly at everything and anything I saw Maga and a couple of my squad taking bullets ,this made me mad I pulled out a grenade and as they approached me I underarm threw it at the truck ,it landed in the rear and I counted to three and saw it erupt in flames killing all aboard instantly

I immediately crossed the street to aid my men when another salvo of mortars came down the blast blowing me off my feet, ,I felt a stinging in my back but I was still mobile so I ignored it, I crawled to Maga and dragged him out of harms way .he was moaning but he was alive, trooper Silvio was lying out in the open and I could see blood pouring from his tunic ,the squad were busy engaging the enemy by returning fire then a second toyota came screaming towards us from the opposite direction guns blazing in all directions I could see that it would run over Silvio again instantly I up and ran at the fallen trooper grabbing him by the shoulders and dragging him a short way off the road while bullets were whizzing all around us.

The toyota passed by us carried on for about twenty more meters skidded and turned a hundred and eighty degrees and started back at us ,the patrol were shooting with everything they had I thought that I was about to die ,I covered Silvio with my body and waited to protect him from further hurt when I heard what I thought was a mortar but instead it was a warrior taking out the truck I raised my head to look and saw the toyota in flames ,the attackers at the rear were jumping off the burning vehicle still shooting, they ran passed me thinking we were dead .I had no weapon to fire as I had dropped it a few yards away when I grabbed Silvio, the last terrorist saw that I was still alive took out his knife to kill me ,as he to had thrown away his weapon when the ammunition had run out when the vehicle was hit ,I put my hand on my kukri withdrew it waited for him to approach ,swiped at his feet and pulled his legs from under him ,he fell heavily and awkwardly at my feet I launched myself at him and cut his throat all in movement of my wrist something I had done many times at Ramadan back home in Nepal, then I blacked out.

I came around in the rear of a landrover being driven to the hospital, my life preserver removed my back now really hurting me the medic heard me moan, I heard him saying "you were a lucky lad son, your flack jacket took the brunt of the shrapnel", you will hurt for a while but a couple weeks recuperation, and you will be ready for action again, of course you will have a few battle scars, and a story to tell your kids.

Captain Keith, informed that they were flying me back to England and that he had written me up for a

George medal, an award that I thoroughly deserved, I have informed your family sergeant, and I will see you when the company returns to the U.K.

The dreadful news chapter 34

Meena was pleased that the shooting of the movie was now complete, she had enjoyed every minute of the experience, the photo shoots," how the people on the computers could eliminate all her self conscious blemishes to make her look "spectacular "in the magazines ". She realized that she had changed, grown in maturity and confidence as the shooting had progressed, she had loved working with her co-star Ganesh, he had encouraged her a lot! with good advice, patience, and handy pointers on her singing and dancing in an industry she was fast falling in love with Nur, called Meena and informed her that Mr. Franklin would like to see her with a view to discussing the final scenes of the film which were now with him,"He is very excited Meena!"He believes that he has a big box office block buster, in" Nan and Kana the movie", he wants to preview it all over the world, I think his ambition is to turn you into an overnight phenomenon, The world exposure would not only be good for you, it would also put his Mumbai studios in the spot light and give him kudos, and untold wealth. and recognition as a director of repute especially in America.

Meena made her way to the Mumbai studios as soon as she had completed showering ,calling Nur to inform her that she was on her way to meet with Franklin , It was about an hour later when her new Mercedes 500sl arrived at her destination ,her first stop was to speak with Nur,to try to get more information as to what her boss was thinking ,Nur said Meena it is all exciting news ,but I prefer that Mr. Franklin tells you himself ,she advised Meena to proceed straight to Franklin,s office ,she knocked on the door ,and waited Franklin opened the door and immediately held out his arms to welcome Meena ,

Meena, welcome! , welcome! "I have good news for you"! , I have completed the final rushes of the film and the full and complete work will go into production immediately, I have been in contact with my opposite number in the UK and they have informed me that the film will be premiered at the Apollo cinema in Hammersmith, London, four weeks from today. Meena!, this, your first musical production will project you into the world spotlight as an international actress of repute, "what do you think of that"? "I am overjoyed sir", replied Meena, Meena this the best production I have ever done and I owe it all to you and your performance, from now on Meena, the world will be your oyster. Mena's hand phone rang, she apologised to Franklin for the intrusion but he encouraged her to answer it, its my mother, Meenas face went pale and she started to shake, tears ran down from her eyes, as her mother conveyed the bad news It's my brother, Rupp, he has been wounded in a bomb explosion in Basra. They are flying him back to England to attend to his wounds, my mother says that he will recover but requires attention that they cannot administer in Iraq, "They are also going to award him with a medal". Meena, my private plane is at your disposal, said Franklin immediately and put his arms around Meena to comfort her, take a deep breath and sit down for a moment, Franklin picked up the phone and asked Nur to come to his office immediately, moments later Nur appeared and was surprised to see Meena in a distressed state, Franklin quickly explained the situation and Nur put her arms around Meena and stroked her hair to settle her down.

After a while Franklin spoke, Meena, I am sending Nur to accompany you to England, but for now I will send her to your room at the Hilton to pack your bags, while she does that I will arrange with my London office to arrange a suite for you at the Kensington Hilton as we have an account with them, we will also locate which hospital they have taken your brother, don't worry Meena, we will do everything humanly possible to make your reunion with your brother a happy one.

Rupp was recuperating in the Shirley oak hospital l in Birmingham when the nurse entered his room, and informed him that he had visitors, Rupp wondered who would be visiting him here, all my comrades are still in Iraq, his jaw dropped when his mother and father accompanied with his sister appeared, "what are you doing here"? He said ", we have come to see our brave son ", said his parents and we have brought your little sister who has made this reunion possible, they all embraced and were thankful that their son was in good hands, while Rupp was in hospital he received a communication from the war office, confirming that he would be presented with his medal by no other than the Queen of England, at a ceremony at the palace six weeks from today, he showed the communication to Meena. Meena assured Rupp, that the family would remain in England to accompany him to receive his award, as they too! had received an invitation accompany him at the ceremony.

For the next two weeks Meena, accompanied by her parents visited Rupp in hospital in Birmingham, until he was released with a full clean bill of health, and ready for further action.

Conclusion

There were thousands of people thronging around outside the Apollo theatre, when Meena and her family arrived, the driver opened the rear door of the limousine to allow Meena to exit, immediately a huge roar erupted, the like she had never experienced, it scared her at first but she stepped out of the limo on to the red carpet and proceeded to wards the entrance, suddenly she was beset with the media asking all sorts of questions, she stopped, saw a little child being crushed by the heaving crowd went over to the barrier and lifted the child to safety, "are you Meena Chandra "asked the child ?yes I am replied Meena ,then can I have your autograph ,of course you can ,the child offered her autograph book and Meena signed it then gave the signature an added bonus by kissing it with her red lips just for you sweetheart just for you, she signed a few more and she slowly moved towards the entrance ,the media continued to press her for answers to their questions Meena reneged and stood beside a young interviewer while all the time the cameras were clicking "Yes this is my first movie, yes It was a wonderful experience working with Ganesh, yes It is my first time in England, so on and so on until she guided her to the entrance, she turned and gave one more wave to the crowd before vanishing inside to be escorted to a reserved seat, the family were already seated and were excited at the prospect of seeing their daughter not anyone else's daughter, but their little girl the star in a Bollywood blockbuster, Rupp sat there with his mouth opened wide, this is my sister, I knew that she could sing and dance, but this was absolutely magnificent far greater than I could ever have imagined she was capable of she has made us so! Proud, after the screening the cast were lined up and introduced to the royal party, the young prince shook Meena by hand and praised her performance, you must be a very talented young lady I no doubt you put a lot of time into making such a wonderful film. I would put money on you to get an Oscar nomination for your performance. Meena smiled and thanked the young prince for his kind words.

The following day the papers raved about the aspiring new Bollywood starlet, comparing her to the Hollywood Greats, Like Marilyn Monroe and Betty Davis, a sure fire Oscar winner in the making, Franklin Pate was also mentioned as one of Bollywood greatest directors.

A few days later after the dust of Meenas screening had settled, in was time to look forward to Rupp's turn to be in the lime light, Meena treated her mother and father to a new set of clothes as she wanted everything to be perfect.

The usher guided the Chandra party to their allotted seats which had a clear view of the parade area the had just settled into their seats when the soldiers that to receive their awards were marched into the parade area, halt, right turn, they all turned in unison to face the officers that were in attendance to her royal highness the royal party made their way to the last soldier, right turned and faced the young warrior The Queen took a medal from a cushion that one of the officers was holding and pinned it on him and shook his hand, her royal highness passed along the line of soldiers to pin their respective honour on to their tunic ,the tears of joy ran down Meenas face as her brother received his medal, how proud she felt we have come a long way from Nepal thought Meena, a long way.

After the ceremony, Meena took her hero brother to one side and said, you know brother your goal of joining the British army and becoming a good soldier like father has been more than exemplified by this honour the queen has bestowed upon you and my dream of Bollywood stardom has been achieved by the Premiering of "Nan & Kana the movie", here in London.

Our parents can be proud of our achievements and they will be secure for the rest of their lives and we have attained our" dreams and aspirations ".

Catterick chapter 4 (appendix)

Situated just a few miles off the Al in North Yorkshire, the base covers an area of some 2,400 acres; with a further 20,000acres of training land .much of this land is designated as a site of scientific interest under the wild life and country act and has the potential for special protection area under a European directive.

As the army's largest base accommodating some 7,500 regular soldiers, 1900 recruits and 2,000 civilian contract workers. Catterick garrison is the standard bearer of the changing face of the modem British army.

The base is the home of 19 light infantry brigade which, although geographically

located within the 2nd division, forms part of 3rd (UK) Division; one of the UKs two deployable divisions .Catterick garrison is also the home for the infantry training where training is conducted for every British and (3hurkha infantry soldier.

Included are the outstations of Ripon, Dishforth, Topeliffe and Marne barracks formerly RAF Catterick, which was handed over to the army in 1994.

Appendix

(The Brecon Beacons so named after the town of Brecon and the ancient practice of lighting signal fires (beacons) on the mountains to warn of attacks from the English.

The Brecon beacons and Elan valley national park spans an area of 519 square miles (1,344 square kilometers). Established in 1957 it is located in mid wales and contains some of the most diverse landscapes in the United Kingdom and Europe.

Sennybridge Training Area (SENTA) consists of some 31, 000acres (l2000ha) of MOD freehold land and 6,000acres of land leased from Forest Enterprise. It measures approximately 12 miles (19 km) SW to NE (8km) SE to NW.

The majority of SENTA is situated on the Mynydd Epynt, a wild plateau covered largely by a blanket bog and grass, but intersected by several stream valleys containing woodland and meadows. these streams provide the main drainage from the Epynt, flowing some five miles (8km) to the river Usk

The uplands of the Epynt plateau lie in the Brecon Beacons to the south and the Cambrian mountains to the north. The area became famous as the breeding ground for Welsh Cobs-the very name Eypnt originating from an ancient expression meaning "haunt of horse". Epynt was the ancestral home of a community of hill farmers until 1940 when it was compulsorily purchased by the war department for use as artillery training area.

The geological features consist of Pen Y Fan, Old Redstone so called due to its distinctive red summit to the south and centre of the area. Much of the upland area is above 1,250 feet (3 80m) with the highest points at the summit Grid (SN 927434) and the Lookout (grid SN961464) at! S33 feet (475m) and 1 S63feet (478m) respectively. Most of the stream valleys lie between 784-899 feet (240-275m)

SENTA is the 3rd largest military training on the UK and in requisitioned in 19391n1940 the Training Area became the site of the Royal Artillery Practice Camp. Since then a wide range of developments have taken place to create live firing and dry training facilities for light forces

Such as the Ghurkha companies and light (195mm) artillery,

All is underpinned by the training camp at Sennybridge which provides the administrative base for units conducting training and the headquarters of the Defence Training Estates Wales & West .The camp can accommodate up to 1760 soldiers)

Afghanistan appendix

Afghanistan stands at the cross roads of central Asia, Afghanistan is proud of having preserved its national identity in the face of the often intrusive interests of other regional powers. The foundation of modern Afghanistan is usually attributed to Ahmad shah Abdali (1947-72) who built an empire in Afghanistan as Mogul power declined in northern India and British influence rose. The Anglo- Russian struggle for influence in Central Asia, the" Great Game, "in the nineteenth century fueled three British Afghan wars in (1839-42, 1878-81 and 1919.For much of the twentieth century successive Afghan governments worked to preserve the independence of the country amidst tumultuous changes: the advances and retreat of European influence in the middle East

The Taliban were already largely isolated .But after 11th September 2001, they came under great international military pressure to hand over Osama Bin Laden. After the fall, of the Taliban regime in 2001, The United Nations brought together leaders of Afghan ethic groups in Germany. The Agreement on provisional arrangements in Afghanistan pending the re-establishment of permanent government institutions (the Bonn Agreement),signed on December 2001, set out the course for the reconstruction and the restoration of representative government in the country.

On October the 9th 2004, Afghanistan held its first ever Presidential elections On Wednesday 3rd November, Hamid Karazi was officially confirmed the winner .This was a significant milestone in Afghanistan's history, and evolution as a *democracy.

Afghanistan possesses a wide variety of mineral resources, including natural gas, coal, oil and gemstones but the security situation has precluded their self effective utilisation.

Drugs, mainly opium dominate illegal exports and, coupled with smuggling to adjacent countries underpin a large black economy.

Britain along with the rest of the international community, are determined never to allow Afghanistan to become a safe haven for terrorists again, and the formulation of the NATO led International Security Force (ISAF), was created for just that reason at the behest of the new Afghanistan government. The 1ST battalion of Royal Gurkha rifles was designated to be deployed to the Helmand area in the south of the country under the operational directive of "Herrick"